THE KANSAS CHRONICLES

THE KANSAS CHRONICLES

Brenda Paske

Writers Club Press
New York Lincoln Shanghai

The Kansas Chronicles

Writers Club Press
an imprint of iUniverse, Inc.

For information address:
iUniverse, Inc.
2021 Pine Lake Road, Suite 100
Lincoln, NE 68512
www.iuniverse.com

ISBN: 0-595-25374-1 (pbk)
ISBN: 0-595-65132-1 (cloth)

Printed in the United States of America

Thanks to Deborah Gouailhardou, for her many helpful comments.

CONTENTS

▼

The Kansas Chronicles

There's stuff that gives you away, like blue eyeshadow, or a mispronounced word.

When Andretta came back from St. Louis for her father's funeral she was driving Paul's Acura, almost brand new. That should have showed them. That should have been good enough.

Andretta was 35, although she looked about 14. She was very little and skinny, with long straight pale brown hair. The whole family was good-looking in that Irish fine-boned way. She was cheerful and friendly and a little outrageous. Her clothes gave it away. She wore patchwork jeans and a headband from the seventies. She hadn't bought anything new in 20 years.

Her little boy came with her from St. Louis. Silent, dark and withdrawn, just like his father. Small for his age, Petey was not a fun child. Paul had insisted he go along. With Andretta's mother in the hospital for foot surgery there was no one to watch him for a week. George, her oldest brother, had broken his wrist. It seemed ridiculous that everyone would all want to be taken care of at the same time. Why should they expect her to do it?

Her mother was finally released from the hospital. They had been worried about some bleeding that wouldn't stop. The old woman was probably faking it to get the attention. She was impossibly demanding. Little Petey was confused and whiny. Andretta escaped to her ex-sister-in-law's house as soon as she could.

Marty went with her. He was her favorite brother, closest to her in age, although she was still six years younger than him. He had tried to commit suicide with some pills four years before, but they never talked about it. The Patersons weren't exhibitionists. They weren't TV talk show material.

✴   ✴   ✴   ✴

"I wonder if Nancy's still as big a bitch as ever," remarked Marty caustically. They both laughed. Nancy was getting well past forty and starting to have that desperate, grasping look. She was small and dark-haired and kept herself in good shape, but her face was hard and her manner brittle. She would never get a man now, not with those two young kids to raise on top of everything else.

Nancy gave them a beer at the door. They hadn't brought anything, they never did. It was funny how everybody seemed to have their little rules for everybody else to follow. But if you just ignored them to begin with no-one tried to push you around.

Nancy introduced her boyfriend Andy, an attractive short red-headed man with an easy-going manner. He and Andretta knew each other already, in a distant way, from before she had moved out of Hutchinson. Andretta left Paul regularly and went home to visit Nancy. Nancy always invited her around during these times. Probably she thought she was doing Andretta a favor. What a pathetic illusion. If Andretta didn't come over she would hardly have any friends at all.

Tonight Andy seemed different. He had sweet blue eyes and a gentle smile. Linda Davis, Andretta's oldest friend, disliked him intensely. "He's totally useless," she had said. "You can just tell. And how could a white man be on welfare for ten years? There's not a thing wrong with him. He just lives off women." Just like Linda to be so judgmental. What gave her the right? She had always been like that, as long as Andretta had known her.

"Get Andretta a chair," snapped Nancy. "Don't just sit there."

Andy smiled when he got it, and touched Andretta's hand.

*   *   *   *

Barbara Davis, Linda's older sister, was back at Andretta's house trying to find her.

"You must come and sit out back, my dear," said Helen, Andretta's mother. "I can't imagine where Andretta is. Petey keeps crying for her. Shame when a mother can't raise her own child. Iced tea?" The tea she gave Barbara smelled like tea. Her own didn't.

"Poor Lawrence, he was such a saint. You know, he was very fond of you."

Barbara smiled politely. The last time she had been over Helen had lurched toward her drunkenly. "I wish the sick old bashthard would die instead of dragging on like this. I'm not a nurse. Why should I be a nurse for the old fool? He never did a thing for me. Just take, take, take."

Andretta said she shouted at him constantly and maybe sometimes hit him. Although she couldn't be sure enough to do anything about it.

"I'm glad to see you turned out so well. You are truly a lovely young lady."

Barbara thanked her.

"You were such a homely, unpleasant little child, you know. You weren't pretty like Andretta. It's nice to see you turned out so well. I've run out of whiskey, do you think you could get me a bottle? Andretta was supposed to. I'll give you the money. If you don't I'll have to go." One foot was still bandaged. "You can just give it to Andretta, she's over at Nancy's. So nice to see you again."

*   *   *   *

They were around the kitchen table when Barbara arrived. "Your mother made me get this," she said. "She wants the change back, too."

"Oh man, she's really unbelievable, isn't she?"

"Petey was wanting you too."

"So?" Andretta shrugged impatiently. "Paul has made him so damned dependant. He tells him awful things are happening to me if he's not right there with me. It's because he doesn't want to watch him for even ten minutes. As long as he keeps the money coming. We haven't slept together for six months. He offered me two hundred dollars to do it with him. I turned him down. I mean, he's really dear and all that but he's almost fifteen years older than me. I don't know why I married him."

She and Andy squeezed hands under the table. Nancy glared, not quite focusing, but knowing something was up. "Why don't you get Barbara a beer?" she said sharply.

"Barbara is my oldest and dearest friend," said Andretta, "I'm glad I'm back. People in St. Louis are so cold. Do you remember Casey? The old lady my parents knew? You knew she shot herself. Well, when I got the news I was so devastated. It was awful. I called up the restaurant where I worked and told them that my best and dearest friend in the whole world had died. They said, like that's real sad. So are you coming to work today?"

"You seem so much more relaxed these days," said Marty to Barbara, offering this compliment like it was a precious gift she had yearned for. "You really have changed. You're so completely serene. What are you doing these days?"

"Oh, working, taking classes, the usual. What about you?"

"I'm between steady jobs. I work nights at a shelter for the homeless. I feel it's my duty."

"That's nice."

"Nice, hell. They're the scum of the earth. Man, I wouldn't even let some of those people touch me. They fall asleep and shit on themselves. They drool and snot runs out of their noses. It's really sick."

"Thanks for the insight, Marty," remarked Nancy.

"We're going to Monica's party in the country. Want to come? Her husband is filthy rich."

"I wouldn't associate with those people," said Nancy. "I hear they're really into drugs and orgies."

"Sounds like fun to me," said Andy. "I think I'll go."

"Go wherever you want," snapped Nancy suddenly. "You're not coming back here if you do. Understood?"

Andy shrugged. "OK, be seeing you." He got up and left. Andretta followed casually.

"So where are you going, you son of a bitch?" screeched Nancy. She ran after them. More screeches from the front yard. Marty and Barbara looked at each other.

"How drunk is she?"

"I'd better go see."

Lights were flicked on in the neighboring yards. Nancy was on top of Andy in the front yard, hitting him with a bottle. Ever the gentleman, he was not hitting back. Blood was running down his head.

A police car pulled up, lighting the scene with a spotlight.

"Let's go," said Andretta, suddenly beside them. They slid out the back door.

*   *   *   *

Later they heard that Nancy had tried to drive away. There was a stiff penalty for DWI, she could have lost her job. The judge sent her to a detox program instead. While she was in the hospital Andy and Andretta lived in her house. When she got out, they left, taking her jewelry and TV. That what she got for being so unreasonable and violent.

Paul came down from Illinois and took Petey with him to stay at his parents. He called Barbara.

"What's going on with Andretta? I know she's living with that guy. I'm ready to forgive her. She doesn't have to worry about that."

Barbara felt irritated. "That's big of you, Paul. Maybe she's ready to forgive you too. I don't recall either of you doing much to keep the family going."

Andretta kept Barbara and Linda supplied with adventure. Hutchinson didn't hold much adventure. Life would be dull without the Patersons. Barbara once had a big thing for Marty. They all seemed so exciting, beautiful and mysterious, back when she was in high school.

"You don't know, Barbara. It's been hard, really hard. You know the way she is. I try to keep Andretta at home. Sometimes she just disappears for days. I take her back, no questions asked. I give her whatever she wants. But this seems serious. This guy, what's he like?"

"Oh, he's a nice guy I guess. Kind of good-looking, but zero personality. He's on welfare."

"Well, they sound like quite a pair. I hope she comes to her senses. I'll let her have her little fling. But I have to protect myself. And my child. Does she seem like a competent mother to you?"

"Frankly Paul, neither of you seem competent. I never saw you spend two minutes with Petey. And where is he right now? With your parents, right?"

"I guess that doesn't look good, does it? I'll get him right back. So would you say Andretta was behaving normally? You know, Petey hasn't asked for her even once since she left."

Barbara could see herself being asked to testify in court. "I'll let you know, Paul."

*   *   *   *

"She turned up on my doorstep absolutely filthy," Linda told Barbara. "You can't even imagine. She said she spent the last two days naked in a van on Monica's farm. Her thighs were just covered with bruises. She said she kept falling down because there were no lights out there."

*   *   *   *

Andretta had gone out there with Marty, her favorite brother. He was the middle child, always the most charming. He and wealthy Monica had had a thing for many years. Marty had explained to her it could never be permanent, she had a good life with her husband. But they would always have deep feelings for each other. Each meeting was bittersweet. They could not come together without thinking of the eventual parting. At least Monica couldn't. At his father's funeral Marty had left the side of the woman he came with to stand by her side. The woman had gone back home soon afterwards. There were others. None so important as her.

Andretta could be a lot of fun, Barbara and Linda agreed. She was the life of every party and told some funny stories. Of course not everyone liked her. She told sad tales of being banned from bars, of people who would not speak to her. Jealous people. Cruel, harsh, judgmental people.

Her first husband beat her. One day when he was working she had posed nude for the artist next door. They were in the front room where there was lots of light. She was standing there, totally naked, and looked up to see, not ten feet away, outside the sliding glass doors, her husband coming home early. He had walked by and never even looked up.

"I'm real messed up by this situation with Paul." She told them. She knew they were jealous of her married to a rich guy in a big city like St. Louis. They had never got out of Hutchinson. They just didn't have her adventuresome spirit. "He's a sweet guy, but I don't know why I ever married him. He's an old man. We have nothing in common. He barely even speaks to me. He has a job playing downtown evenings in some bar. I've only been there once. I'm stuck at home with Petey all day. I mean, I love my kid, but that's no life. I deserve a life. Things can't go on like this."

They nodded and agreed. She should do something about it. Women didn't have to be trapped in bad marriages any more. It wasn't like it used to be.

Barbara, Linda and Andretta, they had been friends for years. Grown up across the street from each other, gone to school together. The Davis family was boring and predictable. Andretta was a little wild, but fun, and marriage had settled her down. The Patersons across the street had been so fascinating. Courtly Mr. Paterson. Beautiful Mrs. Paterson. Their three attractive and witty children, Andretta the only girl. Handsome George, successful Marty. Then Marty had stolen some money from his job. Not a lot of money. They'd kept him out of jail, just barely. Crazed women showed up from time to time to scream at him. Many years later one would shoot, although not kill him. George would be hospitalized briefly for depression, although people said it was drugs. Mrs. Paterson would become a screaming shrew. Mr. Paterson would be dead.

The Davis girls liked to drink. They were big, healthy girls, still fairly athletic. In her younger days Barbara could handle eight drinks in an evening, but now she held it down. Andretta still drank like a fish. Andretta was a little bit of thing, but she could keep up with any man.

Counting later they would agree she had had six beers, a bottle of wine, and four gin and tonics. Linda's husband had to work the next day and went to bed.

Andretta had turned suddenly on Barbara in the middle of conversation. "Well, you wouldn't understand the suffering. You never had any children. You have to be prepared to make the sacrifices of motherhood—you can't just act like the world will give you whatever you want. It's just not that easy."

Barbara shrugged. "Well, I guess it's good I never had kids then. I don't really care for them, to tell you the truth. Not that I dislike them. They're kind of fun for a while. But they're a lot of work."

"Admit it. You just can't deal with real responsibilities. Sometimes you have to give up the things you want. That's life."

Barbara shrugged. She didn't seem to care. She obviously wasn't going to change her life in any real way. It enraged Andretta.

"You just sit up there in your tower and expect the world to fall into place for you. You have to suffer like the rest of us."

"Why should I? It's not like I want a bunch of tiresome responsibilities." Barbara wasn't connecting, probably because she hadn't been drinking like the other two. "Never mind, I'm going to bed."

She left. Linda and Andretta began to talk drunkenly about their glorious high school days.

*   *   *   *

At two o'clock Barbara was awakened by a shout.

"You threw my purse on the roof!" screamed Andretta.

"You're too drunk to drive," said Linda. "You had twice as much as me and I'm too drunk to drive. I'm amazed you can still stand up."

"Bitch! Give me my keys. I want to go home."

"Up yours. You're too drunk."

"Fuck you, bitch. You and your perfect husband and your little prince of a son."

"Go to bed."

"Okay, okay, I'll go to bed. I'll go to bed just like you say."

She walked by Barbara in the guest room, and on into the master bedroom where Linda's husband was sleeping.

"Wake up baby, it's me, your lover. I want to fuck your balls off."

Linda stormed past Barbara in the hall and reappeared dragging tiny Andretta back by the armpits. "Out you go."

She threw her on the bed in the guest room. Andretta bounded up and next door into the kid's room. "Wake up. Wake up, baby. Ooh, you're a cute little princeling."

"That's it, you're out of here."

Barbara dragged herself wearily out of bed.

"Just give me my purse. I want my purse. It's mine," whined Andretta. "You can't keep it. I'll call the police if you don't give it back. You're a thief."

"Go ahead. Call the police. There's the phone. We have serious DWI now in this state. Ask Nancy. Spending the night in jail might do you good."

"I'll drive her," said Barbara. "I have to get home sometime any way." Linda's place was twenty miles out of town and Andretta had driven her over. She got Andretta's purse down from the roof with a broom.

"Goodbye and good riddance," said Linda as they left. "Call me when you make it home, Barb."

At the car Andretta started whining again. "Just give me my keys. I never knew Linda was like that. She must have a really hard life. She's so vulgar and ordinary. What an ugly house. I guess she's jealous. Just give me the keys. I want my keys. It's my car." She wouldn't shut up.

Barbara was shaking from lack of sleep. She grabbed Andretta and shook her. It was like shaking a doll. "Get in the car!" she shouted. To hell with the neighbors.

Andretta got in.

"Wow, I never knew you were like that. You must be really bitter, never having been married and all. Why do you even want to go home? What have you got to go home to?"

"My cat. When I get home I'll get the cat, crawl into the closet and sob like I'm dying over my empty, wasted life." Barbara couldn't seem to start the car. It was a very new model, Paul must have been doing all right.

"You seem to be having a lot of trouble. I think you've had a bit too much to drink. Here, let me drive."

Barbara felt her face reddening, but she controlled herself. "Well, I guess we can just sleep it off here. I can't get it started."

Andretta impatiently unlocked the steering wheel and Barbara managed to start the car.

"You Davis girls are really temperamental. Maybe you shouldn't drink so much."

"Forget it Andretta. It won't work on me. I don't care what you think."

"I know you're just concerned, but this is really co-dependant of you. I'm OK now, I'm ready to drive." Andretta was digging in her purse.

"Well you're not going to. You're going home."

"What do you mean, home? You mean my mother? What the hell makes you think I want to go there?"

"Fine. So where do you want to go?"

"I want my car. It's my car. I want to drive."

"Forget it."

Suddenly Andretta was all over Barbara. She'd found another set of keys somewhere in her purse and attacked Barbara's arm with them. They wrestled for the steering wheel, wavering wildly and finally ending up in the opposite lane pointed the wrong way. Barbara slammed Andretta in the stomach with her elbow.

"Cut it out, you bitch!" Barbara shrieked. "Or you're dead."

There was dead silence while Andretta caught her breath.

"Have you ever considered mental help?" asked Andretta sweetly.

"Fuck you."

"You're so abusive. Where are you going? This isn't the way home."

"We're going to my place. I can't drive you any further. You can't be trusted."

"You have a lot of little rules, Barbara. A lot of petty little rules that don't make much sense to anybody anymore. Nobody cares. You can't control your own life, why are you trying to control mine? Why don't you just give it up?"

Barbara ignored her.

"You're just not on our level, Barbara. We're not like you Davis's. We have class. We're something special."

"You're far from ordinary, that's for sure."

"You know, the light in this car makes you look older than I've ever known you, Barbara. You're all used up. Don't you know how meaningless your life has been? It has no point. There's no joy in it. You know, Marty's never loved you."

"Oh dear. I'll go home and take sleeping pills."

"You look really haggard. It's too bad you didn't get a man while you were still young. Now you're old and you have nothing and you never will have anything."

Barbara pulled up in front of her apartment complex and they got out.

"You can't come in."

"I don't want to come in."

"Fine. I'm calling somebody to come and get you."

"Go ahead. I have another set of keys." She was prepared for this, Barbara realized in a flash. Prior experience. She wrestled Andretta's purse from her and dumped it out. She snatched up the third set of keys.

Andretta followed Barbara across the parking lot wailing like a tiny lost dog, for the benefit of the whole complex.

"Give me my keys back. I just want my keys back. They're mine. I want them back. Give them back. You bitch!"

"Shut up or I'll call the police."

"Call them. You gave me a black eye. I'll file charges."

She pointed at a perfectly healthy eye. Had Barbara managed to smack it in their struggle? Barbara felt chilled. It was all too pat. Who knew how many times she'd done it before?

"I'll call your brother to come get you."

She went in and dialed, listening with one ear as Andretta kept wailing. He answered sleepily. "Listen Marty, this is Barbara. I'm at home. I think you'd better come and get Andretta."

He hung up on her.

"I found your car, bitch. I'm going to break the windows you butch, pervo lesbian."

A police car pulled up. Apparently someone in the building wasn't sleeping well.

They took Andretta aside and talked to her. One officer came over to Barbara.

"Uh, miss, I think you'd better give the car keys back."

"Fine, you take them. I won't be responsible."

"Sorry. You did the right thing. It's just that we can't do anything unless they're actually driving erratically. We'll follow her little bit and see if she's all right."

Apparently she was. Linda called Andretta's mother the next day. Andretta had gotten home early in the morning. "But Barbara certainly has a vicious temper," Helen said. "Have you thought of getting her some help?"

*   *   *   *

Andretta sat sadly in the kitchen with her mother. She thought of her dear, sweet, dead father. The paper had a wonderful obituary. She had forgotten what a wonderful man he was. It was easy. In the last ten years he had declined so badly.

"You father was a bahshtard," said her mother. "You children never knew what a bahshtard he was."

She sighed. Once a month around midnight her mother called her and gave her this speech. She gave it to one of her children on a weekly basis. In between she called what friends she had and gave it to them.

"He never did a thing. Not a thing. He just sat up in his study like it was his kingdom. He didn't know a thing of what I had to go through.

I could have been a doctor if it weren't for that bastard. Now he's dead, but it's too late. My life is over with and I sacrificed ten years of it taking care of him. That SOB husband of yours called. I told him to leave you alone. He's a bashtard too. Your child is not safe with him. He's a strange little man, Andretta. You should get your child away."

"He has to learn sometime, Mom. Too many years I let him get away with it. He never took care of Petey for more than two hours. I was out with friends once and he took him right into the bar to take me back home. Well, now he has to learn. I'm not doing everything. I had to go to work just to buy myself a new dress. He wouldn't give me any money, not even for a dress. He makes four thousand a month and he never gave me any money."

"Well, that will change now, honey. You've got him changing. But what's going to change for me? It's too late for me. Look at my life. I have nothing. Nothing. It's all I'll ever have."

"You have the insurance money."

"What can I do with it? I have no friends. No hopes, no dreams. My health is shot. I might as well be dead."

*   *   *   *

"She's so depressed," said Andretta to Andy. "She's really hurting. My Mama. If only there was something I could do for her." She opened another bottle of beer. "She drinks like a fish. I don't think she can stop. It will probably kill her. She's practically crippled. She can't drive anywhere. I would hate to live like that. She told me she would be better off dead."

"Do you think she'll try anything?" asked Andy. "I know a lot of people who killed themselves. It's real bad, man. It's a real bad state of mind."

"I don't know. You know she still drives that car sometimes. Anything could happen. She needs someone to look after her. It's just so hard though. I try to help people all the time. But they never do any-thing for me."

"People are so selfish," agreed Andy.

*   *   *   *

Andy's disability money was steady, and Andretta got a little bit of money from Paul every month. He still called occasionally, trying to get her home. She paid for gas with his credit card, and bought Andy a stereo.

"I've got to be on my own for a while," she told Paul. "It's just something I have to do."

"You're living with that man, aren't you? What kind of a mother are you?"

"Don't you dare spy on me, you SOB." she screamed. "Don't you dare tell me how to run my life. Don't you dare use my own child against me."

"Just remember I'm always here," he said, before he hung up. Nei-ther of them mentioned Petey again.

Still, it would be nice to have more money. It was Andy who sug-gested it.

"Your mom is all alone in that big house. She really needs help. I don't think your brothers will do it. Do you think she'd pay me a sal-ary? Like for being a handyman or something? She really needs one. I used to do it for an apartment complex."

Andy was not a bum. He was not as materialistic as some guys and that made certain people look down on him. But he was a nice guy. Lots of guys in five hundred dollar suits couldn't say that. He was lov-ing and friendly and liked to have a good time with Andretta. So what was wrong with that?

He fixed the shed for her mother. "You're a lazy bahstard, Andy," Helen would tell him. "You're living off of Paul, you know that don't you? Another man's money."

"I have disability coming in," Andy would remind her.

"Yeah mom, Andy always worked real hard, but when he got hurt they laid him off like he was nothing. Andy would work, it's just that he can't. He fixed up the shed real nice back there. Got a lock on the door and everything. He keeps things real nice around the house for you. I think you ought to pay him."

"I do pay him. He eats my food and sleeps in my house and spends his disability on liquor and drugs. I had fifty dollars in my bureau Wednesday morning, but now it's gone. What would you know about that?"

Andretta had had to borrow a little something. "I took it for the groceries, don't you remember?"

"Don't you take money out of my bureau for your worthless gigolo man, girlie. I won't have stealing."

"Nobody stole anything, you just don't remember, you old witch. You ought to be paying us a salary. We take care of you night and day. You drink up all your money. Probably you'd die in a house fire if we weren't here. You always smoke in bed."

"I don't need your help, Missy. You need help. Mental help. Leaving that sweet adoring husband for this cheap piece of trash. Why my father would not have had him in the house." She waved a carving knife at Andy. "Out of here, you trash. I want you out of this house."

Andy backed away toward the door. "Yes ma'am, whatever you say."

Andretta wrestled with her mother. "You crazy old woman! Give me that! I'll have you put away!" She got the knife away from her. "You pay us what you owe us! Andy did a hundred dollars worth of labor on that shed and that's cheap. You hand it over. You got your check yesterday. I know you've got it."

She ran up the stairs and started throwing clothes out of the drawers. "You tell me where you left my money!!"

Helen hobbled after her, but caught sight of Andy again. "You! Get out!" She shrieked. "Get out of here. I'll call the police." She snatched open the door, shouting "Help! Help! Call the police!"

There was a short hedge in front of the house and nobody seemed to notice much. Some black boys up the block playing basketball turned to look, but turned back away when they saw what house was causing the commotion.

Andretta raced back down the stairs and got the door shut. "SShhh. SSHHH. Can't you keep her quiet? The police will be here, man."

Andy smiled weakly. "It's her house."

"Mom, calm down. The neighbors will think you're crazy. We don't need that. Now just be quiet. I think we all need a little drink."

Helen got a cunning look in her eye. "Why don't you fix us some gin and tonic, dear. I think I will go down in the basement and collect my knitting to calm me down."

Andretta watched her go with a little smile. "She thinks I don't know about the shotgun down there, but I do. I took it down to the pawnshop last week. Hah."

She fixed two drinks. "Settle down, I'll get the money."

There was a crash and cursing from down in the basement.

"She sounds mad," ventured Andy.

Andretta got up and locked the basement door. "She'll calm down. I am sick of being treated like this. You worked hard. You deserve the money. You need to stick up for yourself more. Look at these bruises the old witch gave me. I think I will see a lawyer. Would you say she was incompetent?" Paul used that word a lot. It must mean something legally serious.

"I'm not a doctor."

There was a ranting string of curses, then a crash, and silence.

"That'll learn you, you old boozy witch," yelled Andretta. "No, don't go down. It'll only get her started again. If she got herself in a mess she can get herself out of it."

"Maybe she's hurt."

"She's not yelling for help is she? She's just got to learn to treat you better. I wonder where she put the money."

She went upstairs for a while. "I found it. In her shoe. She probably doesn't remember herself. Here. It's yours. Be a sweetie and buy us another bottle of gin."

"This is two hundred bucks. Let's have some fun."

They were out all night. Barbara saw them at the Gold Rush, but turned away with a shrug. Other old friends were there. Monica and her husband. "How's Marty, Andretta?" she asked wistfully. Andy bought a couple of rounds.

"Andy got paid tonight. We're celebrating. We're going to get married real soon."

Andy looked embarrassed.

"Andy will be taking care of some properties around town. Mom said today she'd help him start his business."

They got home early in the morning and went straight to bed.

*   *   *   *

Andretta woke up first and went down to make some coffee. Usually Helen was padding around sleeplessly in her robe and slippers by now, banging cabinet doors to wake them up. The basement door was locked, Andretta remembered suddenly.

"Oh shit. Mom?" She opened the door. No answer. "Shit. Damn." She went down the stairs cautiously. "Mom? Oh my God!"

Helen was lying in a rusty pool under the old metal tool shelves. Andretta ran back upstairs and shook Andy awake.

"Andy! Get downstairs. Mama's not moving!"

"Eh? What?" He looked confused and slow. She had never noticed before that he looked so stupid.

*   *   *   *

Helen didn't look any better from Andy's point of view on the stairs. Andretta refused to go down.

"I think she's dead."

"Oh, no no. What do we do?"

"Call an ambulance."

"She's dead. I know she's dead. What do we tell them?"

"It was an accident. She always drank a lot. She had an accident."
Andy dialed 911.

✳   ✳   ✳   ✳

The police came with the ambulance.

"You seem to have bruises on your arm, Miss."

"There was a fight." The officer waited. Andretta felt very nervous suddenly. She didn't want to talk about her mother. Everybody would hate her. "I—It wasn't really a fight. Sometimes Andy doesn't know what he is doing. It didn't hurt really. Don't say anything to him, please."

She looked about sixteen, standing there in an man's old workshirt and shorts.

"Did your mother get along with him?"

"Well, mostly. She owed him some money I guess, but he finally got it last night." She started to cry.

Everything had gone all wrong. It was Andy's fault, really. Couldn't he figure out how to do anything? It was all messed up. Couldn't they see it was all messed up? Somebody had to fix things. They couldn't expect her to live like this.

Somebody had better fix it now.

In the Sink

You aren't careful, her momma had told her, you gonna end up in the sink. Which was her way of saying—in the toilet.

June, the man's no damn good. And what about that woman and her kid? You know it's his. I know you do. You been lazy, plodding along, not lifting a finger, letting what comes come. Letting everything else just go. You don't make an effort, see, but someday you will.

Momma had sent the carrot tops shooting into the sink with her knife blade to emphasize. Turned the water on, then the garbage disposal. Old withered arms quivered in her short-sleeved blouse. It was nicely ironed, like June's own clothes never were.

And didn't her momma's words come back like a curse.

You're going along, all of a sudden—boom. You're in the sink. Screaming and kicking your feet. Fighting and clawing your way back.

A bit of carrot was coughed back up out of the sink. She shoved it back in. The sink growled.

And all for nothing. The best you can hope for is to get out of the sink. And that's the best. That terrible effort you finally put forth, it might have been turned to something useful. But instead it just gets you back out. If you even can do so much.

What an old witch. Doug had said that about her momma, scratching his hairy belly. Just like her ugly daughter.

So why did she think of that now? It was the noises in the downstairs toilet.

Katie had slammed the lid down quick. "Yuuucckkk. Mommmmm."

June lifted the lid. Blood. No doubt about it. Red and dark as a miscarriage and a truly disgusting gurgling noise from somewhere deep in the pipes.

"Well, for God's sake, use the one upstairs until I can get the plumber." Which would cost 80 bucks, maybe more, and the car needed tuning.

"But Mom, what is it?"

"Rust. Rust backing up from the pipes. Just what I need. Whiny kids and a rusty toilet."

Not a haunt. Not someone who couldn't stay dead.

June had a friend, Susie, when they were both 16. They skipped school, were sitting around in Susie's kitchen, smoking a jay as it rained outside.

"Susie, Susie, there's a cat stuck up in your tree." Which there was, a grey and black stringy looking cat, wet and unattractive, perched up there way back, yowling its fool head off in a rage, didn't want to come down. Of course in the end they do, how many times you been walking in the park, noticed the pathetic dried-up skeletons high in the trees, of cats that wouldn't come down?

Susie got up, cute and blonde as she was, with big blue innocent eyes. She got down her daddy's shotgun, went out back and blasted that cat right out of the tree.

This is a true story. About a girl with what you would call a practical turn of mind.

"Mommy, mommy, mommy." It was a chant, almost a song, not scared yet. The girls were looking out back, into the lashing Kansas rainstorm. "There's a dog out under that tree."

It looked like the neighborhood mutt. Standing under the cottonwood, wet clear through and mangy, and his eyes glowed blue.

"It's just old Petey."

"Look at his eyes, Mom."

"It's just the storm. You girls get to bed. Quit fooling around. I ain't got time."

Work, the girls and the house. There was never time or energy. One thing about the unemployed, they always had plenty of both. It was like fighting a zombie, always coming back from the dead. Now Doug was gone, things were actually better.

Used to not asking questions, the girls went to bed. They didn't bother brushing their teeth.

After the divorce, Doug had taken all the guns, probably sold them, although he did leave one. She hadn't bought another. It would have seemed suspicious somehow. Instead she kept an ax in her bedroom. When she felt the pressure of bad thoughts around her she would hold it in her hand, heft it this way and that. She would think of Lizzie Borden, who never did get hung. People always forgot about that part when they told the story.

The screen door slammed behind her. She walked across the concrete patio, onto the wet grass. Lots of people were scared of storms, but personally she liked them.

The dog growled at her, it wasn't Petey, and she sure hoped the neighbors weren't watching when she chopped off his head. It was not a clean job, but there was no blood, of course. Because it wasn't really a dog. She buried him in a corner of the garden with a few extra smacks of the shovel.

"Take that, dickhead." She could deal with it. Men harden themselves to war, enjoy it too. But women are supposed to be a different species. The nurturing ones.

"Nurture some worms," she muttered.

Back into the house, she saw herself in the hall mirror, white-faced, frizzy-haired, pock-marked, caught like a woman on trial.

Doug was gone. To be fair, to do him justice, she had to admit that nobody cared. If only somebody had cared, maybe he could have cared back.

When the little girl from the other side of town disappeared, somebody cared. For a month it was on the news and neighbors searching everyday. A wan-faced manic-depressive mother of two vanished and was in the newspaper for two weeks until she was found to have drowned herself. The little girl turned up dead in the end too.

Merely mention, however, the child support issue, and eyes cloud over, lawyers blink, officers edge away and nod impatiently. It fit the pattern. Of course he's gone, far away, never to be found. Like magic, nobody bothered to look further, into an empty field, littered with beer cans, someways to the west.

The hardest thing is a pattern. You cannot break it. The lies, the drinking, the rages, the unemployment. Once you see it, the best you can hope for is a shift. Don't bother hoping for a miracle, don't pray or try to understand. All you can do is make it something else, something everybody knows. But you must be quick. And you must know what pattern.

They're too young to know, Cindy is 6, with her daddy in her, all the weak parts. They don't look too bad on a woman, lucky her. Katie is 10 and a nervous one—but she sees more than she says. It's good to keep your own thoughts to yourself. And hasn't she had practice.

Her girls will be women someday, and doesn't every woman see enough blood almost each and every month to make a small yet hideous tragedy? Don't some fancy dainty manners fool you. Why paint your nails red, if not for a warning?

Lydia came over the 4th of July. Neighbor woman, sixty years old, husband dead of Parkinson's, and harassment. She drinks a lot, was pretty once, maybe sees that black hole in front of her that June sees every night, can barely stand to sleep without a light, now. Yes, sometimes she wakes up and has to turn it on.

"I never thought you'd come to any good, June, but you have those fine girls. Get me some whiskey, dear, or I'll have to go get it myself. Hard to see at night with these old eyes. How have things been with you?"

"Doug ran out on the child support. It hasn't been easy."

'Doug' was one letter off from 'Dog', she realized. 'Dog' without 'u'.

"Better off without him." Lydia sucked in her whiskey. "You're lucky, women today. Why, I could have been a lawyer myself, if that bastard hadn't held me back."

"Men are dogs."

"Dogs are faithful." They laugh. Out of the corner of her eye she sees a dog's brown butt, tail waving. It's behind some bushes. She doesn't see the head. It's shadowy there in the back yard, but still, there should be a head.

Katie's looking thoughtful, pretending not to see. Cindy's watching her sparkler, waving it happily, like a normal kid again.

After everyone's gone to bed, she tracks down the headless carcass, sprinkles firecracker dust over it, lights it and sends it galloping down the street with a good boot in the rear. Cheerful as any Kansas farm girl on a hot summer night.

Get them drunk enough, they all take their clothes off. Doug had said that. We all know how it's done. Works the same with a man. They always take their clothes off before they off themselves. Somebody in police dispatch had told her that. Guess they figure they're going back to their mommas the same way they came in.

No Humane Society for sick dogs in the country, you just shoot them in the head. You've seen it done, and this is no different. Easier even.

Just don't look. Driving off fast on the sandy road, not in a panic, just trying not to think, she hit a dog. A real one. Hit it and kept on going. Didn't stop to put it out of its misery.

Even she had to admit, that just wasn't right.

Katie looks thoughtful, licks her lips. "Petey's in the closet," is how she puts it.

The kids clothes are a mess on the floor, greyish stuff dribbled all over them, and was it going to wash out? Her grandma's house smelled like that after she died. Sweetish. Kind of nasty, but not bad like you would think. Not good, either.

The dog's head is in the closet, snarling spittle and hanging by his teeth from Cindy's brand new sweatsuit. She ties pajama arms smartly around his jaw, so he can't bite. Marches down to the kitchen and wraps the head in Saran wrap. Some dim idea of smothering it was in her mind. She would like to incinerate it somehow, and run it through the trash compactor, but thinks perhaps it would return in a different form, maybe a plague of angry rats or stinging beetles, like an LSD flashback that never went away. The thing doesn't breathe, of course, wasted effort, the Saran wrap, but she wraps around and around until she has a great glistening Saran ball.

"Mom?"

"Just cleaning up." she says grimly. She can handle it.

She rolled the ball down the basement steps. Heard the thuds as it started rolling around the dark by itself.

"I don't believe you girls should play down there any more," she heard herself say. Thud, thud, thud. She wondered what it was like, wrapped in plastic, knows she will dream of it tonight, blind and smothered. Eventually, of course, it would unroll itself and she would have to take further steps.

"But MOM."

"Go outside and play" she snapped. "It's for your own good. You'll understand when you're older."

It all evens out in the long long run. What you take, you don't always have to pay for right away. Not right away, and not all at once. Like a credit card, just take the misery a little at a time.

Put off that day, month after month. That day when you look at the final balance, when you have to look and see what you have done.

SISTERS

The street people weren't so bad that winter. Maybe they had all died off in the bitter cold. It made Melissa hold her breath all the way to the subway stop, so that none of that bone-chilling death would get inside her. Wrapped in her cloth coat that did not look stylishly bedraggled, she wondered how anyone could survive long in that wind. It was so cold you couldn't even dream of warmth, couldn't believe in it, couldn't have faith that you would again know Spring.

Perhaps someone had done something about the situation. Taken the street people in hand, transported them all to uncarpeted dormitories, with threadbare blankets and uncurtained windows. A world of cold toast, grey-green paint, stopped-up toilets and a single fuzzy black and white TV tuned eternally to Wheel of Fortune.

At least in the winter the smell wouldn't be so bad. The circulation in their feeble old hands would slow to the point that even a parasite couldn't survive decently. Mottled claws trembling over each other in the dim light. Because even inside, out of the wind, the cold slowly creeps back. Just when you should be getting warmer it became apparent you were really getting colder. The rapid metronome of shivers had stopped, but deep in your bones, a slower, more deadly clock was ticking.

Annette was gone on a long ski vacation with Dave, and Melissa was left alone in the underfurnished apartment with its hollow-sounding wooden floors. All of empty February she lay in her blankets next to her reading lamp that she never dared turn off. Shivering and alone. The quiet was all about her, as if there were no one left in the city, in their little concrete rooms. As if she were all alone in a little circle of lamplight in the early snowy dark. Evacuation. Air Raid. The sirens had gone off and somehow she hadn't heard.

She didn't call anyone, determined not to be one of those panic-stricken females who clutch at the first thing remotely human in their reach. Would she tell them anyway? How could she explain the fear?

One night she woke with the memory of a scream.

Across from them lived the Wartmans. Heidi, and Junior, her son. Heidi stumped slowly up and down the stairs to collect the mail and sometimes to sit in the park.

There had once been a Mr. Wartman. No one had illegitimate children in Heidi's day. Wartman Senior was long gone, it seemed.

And Junior was tired of the situation. He could be heard threatening to kill his mother, calling her a useless old bitch, slapping her.

Annette would yell out the window, "Hey, shut up. We're trying to sleep, OK? You ought to be ashamed, talking to your mother that way."

And Wartman Junior would never yell back. He would shut the window quickly and pull the shade and keep doing whatever it was.

But Annette was gone. Melissa was left alone to decide. Did Mrs. Wartman scream? Had she been murdered in the night? Who would know? She was gone, but where to? An old folk's home? If Annette were there she would have known what to do. "Hey Wartman, where's your mom?" She would have asked, passing him on the stairs. Junior's eyes would have darted about and settled furtively on her collarbone and he would croak out some obvious lie that would unmask him. Say that she was in bed sleeping, recovering from a stroke. Her bleary old eyes wandering over the cracked yellow plaster of the ceiling. When everyone could clearly see that her bed had been empty day after day. Nervous lies, that would destroy him.

Give it time, and the disease that had his mother would someday have him too. One by one the cells were already flickering out and not being replaced. The eyes blurred, the hands shook, the mind turned aimlessly in the same path. You had to take what you could, deserving or not, because you could never be better.

Wartman after Wartman, the one dead, the other living, pursuing each other endless down the halls of winter. Perhaps he'd smothered her in the dead of night. For the insurance money maybe. Would he ever brood about it? Would it haunt him? When his legs were veined and shaky would he remember? Or was it nothing, a relief from a bother, a pest, a whining old woman who babbled like some deranged old parrot, about nothing, nothing at all.

Imagine growing old, seeing only those people who saw you too, alive to only a few of the living. Yes, it would be a deserted city then, empty as the desert, the vultures wheeling.

And even Junior would not watch, late at night, as she wandered from room to lighted room, wearing an old T-shirt as a nightgown.

When Annette came back, things were already back to normal. Wartman Junior had moved the week before. The wind had died down, the sky was fresh and bright. Melissa told her about the Wartmans.

"Good riddance," said Annette, shrugging thoughtlessly. "That pair always made a racket."

Months later Melissa still remembered at odd times, in strange places.

On a subway ride with Annette and Jonathan she had doubts. She had felt these vague doubts all through the long subway ride through progressively worse neighborhoods, deep into the kingdom of despair.

The inhabitants that ventured below the earth cared nothing for themselves. Original Stoics, time-transported straight from Rome, that wasted no time on vanities. Scabby faces, swollen hands, dirty nails, clothes that had obviously molded themselves to someone else's shape long before their time at the Salvation Army. Bought as coverings, upholstery, to cover broken springs, torn seat cushions, exposed stuffing. No style, no self-expression. They shoved themselves sullenly in and out of the cars. There was no air-conditioning of course. All of the graffiti was smeared in uniform black on toothpaste green walls. The windows were opened and the train rattled wearily along, making knocking noises as if the Wartmans below wanted to come in. The subways go through Death's kingdom.

Annette didn't seem to notice. She leaned back comfortable, long bare legs stretched out, talking to Jon only occasionally, because of the noise of the train. She wasn't worried at all.

Fools are the children of God.

And what did they know about Jonathan after all? Annette had met him at the city swimming pool. It could as easily have been the gym. She tended to her body as easily as other people brushed their hair.

Melissa had gone there with Annette one day. Jon had glanced at her without interest and said a few polite things. Hadn't even bothered to show off, as he followed Annette with his eyes, swimming steadily up and down the lanes.

She had once been considered the pretty one. Annette was too long and scrawny, like a boy. Now Melissa was pallid and uninteresting, washed out in any light. Not old, but nearly thirty, she had lost that certain fresh stupidity of the young.

Well, Jonathan was no prize himself, although men always thought they were somehow. He swam adequately, or Annette would never have bothered to speak with him, but he was pale. Too pale for a dark-haired man. Pale people always looked a little swollen, unless they were small-boned like the Irish. He had big hands though, strong. A little womanish in the face, a nineteenth century type. His bristly mustache looked unreal on his sensitive, old-fashioned face. Too well tended. Silly vanities were more appealing in women somehow. She was sure he spent hours combing and clipping the shrubbery. Soulful eyes, wistful and weakly blue, a red mouth. And Annette, strong and spare, with the cheekbones of a Russian countess.

Why waste her time? He worked in a bookstore and lived with his mother. She could have stockbrokers at the very least. Why did she always take the whiners?

The last one had sculpted, blow-dried and backcombed his hair to perfection every morning. The operation had tied up the bathroom forty-five minutes a day, every day. At least he had moved in, rather than Annette moving out. Every other night at two o'clock the phone would ring as some old girlfriend of his would be in need of comfort. The original opportunist. If you were ready, he would be too, without fail.

The most persistent girlfriend had actually picked up his laundry for him at the apartment. Eventually he had moved in with her.

A string, a short string of little men with stunted minds. Annette allowed them to claim ownership. Without the self-respect to think of their property as valuable, they soon left. And not without a parting shot or two at Melissa.

"Your sister gives me the creeps. Lesbo man-hater." Some form of that was common. Annette never noticed how many of them said it. She really didn't seem to care.

The end of the line was outside a row of squatty, double-locked and gated businesses. The bus ride was thirty minutes. Jon assured them it was worth the unspoiled beach, Melissa didn't even know where she was. Annette didn't either, she was sure. She couldn't even guess. They were relying on Jon.

It was seven o'clock when the bus stopped. If only they'd gone on the weekend, at some decent hour. It was a long ride back to the city and it would be late.

They got off the bus in the middle of a field, carefully clipped, but totally empty except for some bushes in the far distance and a maintenance hut. She could not hear the sound of the waves, or glimpse the ocean.

At least there was a breeze, out in the open. Strange how the heat made people visible to her again, the millions of them in the city, like cockroaches crawled out overnight and here to stay.

It was a long walk across the field and her pack was heavy with books. She let it cut into her hand, then twist her fingers, then pull her shoulders out of alignment.

How far was it? Annette and Jon strode on ahead, Jon talking in a nauseatingly intimate voice. He didn't offer to carry Melissa's pack. A feminist, no doubt.

Behind the bushes were three cinderblock houses with no glass in the windows and no doors. Anyone could have been inside. Murderers. Drug addicts. Jon and Annette didn't even glance twice at them. And beyond, the sand. And the beach, after all. The lifeguard's chair was held by somebody obviously not a lifeguard, with his family in tow. There were only three other people chatting, far down the beach, under a darkening, cloudy sky.

"It might rain," she ventured.

They looked at her blankly. Annette had worn her suit under her clothes, but Jon changed behind their backs, in the open air. He could have used one of the buildings, thought Melissa. He had nothing much to show. Just long dark hairs on his pale scrawny legs. Annette ignored them both and watched the waves.

The sky was truly dark. It must be eight at least. Melissa rolled up her jeans and waded into the foam.

"There's a nice club up the beach, they'll let us in in our suits. How about it? Why don't you change?" asked Jonathan. He sounded a little eager. He was wearing a ridiculously tiny little red groin cover. Melissa averted her eyes and tried not to laugh.

"I didn't bring a suit. I thought I'd just wade."

"You didn't bring a suit?" he asked incredulously, as if he'd caught her with her hand on his wallet. "Well what did you come out here for, then?"

"To enjoy the beach." She was prepared for that one.

"Well, I came to swim," he said huffily.

"Let's do it then," said Annette and hopped cheerfully into the ice cold waves without any hesitation. Jon stared after her, then followed, a little gingerly.

The jerk.

"It gets warmer once you're in," said Annette. "Come on, you don't need a suit."

Melissa shook her head and looked at the sky. Ships winked their lights miles offshore.

"Soviet trawlers," explained Jon. "Right at the three mile mark."

Of course. Soviet trawlers. She personally couldn't see three miles in the dark.

Would it rain? If a bolt of lightening hit would it kill them all like the fish? She at least would flop down in shallow water, and if only stunned, would not drown terribly, paralyzed and helpless.

The man who was not a lifeguard left, along with his family. A black couple, with a huge dog, probably trained to attack, walked slowly and safely down the beach.

Jon and Annette swam the other way, taking a very long time and finally disappearing. If there was an accident in the dark, who would save them? She thought of the long walk over the field, the empty houses, the bus from nowhere. But Jon had said there was a club up the beach. She imagined them in their wet suits, sitting at the bar, having some silly pink drink, changing into the clothes that Jon kept there, he knew the place after all, catching the bus, heading back into town. Jon laughing secretly at her and what he imagined was her silly plot to ruin things, sitting there all alone in the gloom, watching their things. Annette would merely have forgotten. They would be angry at her if she didn't bring everything back, and try to make out it was all her fault.

You must have known we weren't coming back. How long did you wait, anyway?

If some useless woman must tag along, why then she should carry the luggage.

In suppressed panic she watched the waves as it got darker and finally became night. Somebody got out of the grey water further down the beach, but it wasn't Annette after all.

Perhaps he'd pulled her under. Who knew how sane he was? That's why he'd gotten her up the beach, away from help. That's why he'd been angry that Melissa had come. That's why he had separated them. He could never have fought them both off. Melissa was the sensitive one, she'd cry and be upset when he told her her sister was gone, instead of knowing instantly what to do. All alone with him. She imagined his pale hairy arms around Annette with disgust. His anger at her lack of responsiveness. Thinking, why should he put up with it?

She could imagine the false sympathetic smile on his face. The damp bulging eyes. "Annette's not with you? But she went back a half hour ago." The worried wait, his eyes stealing glances at her misery, something in her knowing the truth. Something in him savoring it. She would want to leave, get help, but he would protest that she was over reacting until it was far too late. They would walk down the beach calling, he would say, "Perhaps. she did us a favor, leaving us alone together."

It was contempt behind it all. Contempt for what they thought she was. And the bland lies when they accidentally burned holes in your favorite sweater, spilled greasy food in your books, locked the cat out. Suggesting there was something wrong with you for noticing, paranoid, neurotic. What's your problem Melissa, I mean, exactly what?

What if Annette changed? Thought nothing of cleaning up and cooking for a man who really loved her? Whatever thoughts she had immediately becoming invisible in the glare of a man's attention. There's no point in being bitter, in dwelling on the past. Maybe you should try harder to make yourself attractive. Staving off her own day of reckoning with nervous laughs and lies.

Annette was not like that, somehow she had been spared. She took Melissa's statements calmly, maybe even not understanding. Never protested or advanced opinions of her own. She had none.

At nights, when she was young, Melissa would look at shadows on the wall of her bedroom and think I, I myself will be dead someday, dying all alone in some hospital room. Suffocating, knowing it was the end, the flickering light gone at last, forever. Everyone she knew gone. None of them knew her, really. Everyone was strange to her but Annette.

The water lapped at her toes, rushed over her ankles, to her knees. Splashed her jeans.

There would never be a man good enough for Annette, would there? It didn't matter to Annette now, but maybe she couldn't see the pattern.

Saturday mornings they would do their laundry and let the cats out in the park a while. Melissa would fix brunch, she liked to cook, and they'd drink champagne cocktails with their friends. They would read the paper and maybe go to the beach, with the crowds and in the bright sun which illuminated them all.

Finally it was utterly dark. No lights on the beach, of course. A few distant lights twinkled in the mowed field. They only showed how deserted it was.

She imagined a running figure, going for help, caught and framed by the solitary lights. The vast distances made it seem hardly to move. Precious time streaming away as it crept to the first light, the second, the bike path, the road.

Jon sulked, and lit another cigarette.

"We'll leave in a minute," he assured her heartily. She was happy to ignore the signs of baffled male frustration. "I'm sure that relieves you. You must have been terribly bored."

Melissa shrugged, not caring. The breeze was a little sharp, but with Annette back she could have stayed on.

They sat a while, watching the twinkling lights offshore. It was much more than a few minutes when Jon asked Annette if she was ready to leave.

"I guess, how about you?" She spoke to Melissa, but Jon answered.

"Oh, I'm fine. I'm perfectly happy. The weather's beautiful. I could stay here all night." The sarcasm of his tone did not penetrate to Annette. Melissa heard the calculation underneath it all. He had been planning to stay, if she had not been along. And what could Annette have done about it? She didn't know the way back.

They pulled together the towels and blankets and crossed the boardwalk, Jon lagging. This annoyed Melissa. She didn't know which way to go. Where was the bus stop this side of the park?

"This way," said Jon. He led them down a bike path.

"Is this the way we came?" asked Annette, looking about vaguely in the dark.

"No," said Melissa immediately.

Jon sighed loudly.

They heard muttering. At first Melissa thought it was a trick of the ocean, but then she saw the figures by the beach house. There were eight or nine of them, squatting and smoking.

Haitians, she thought. Boat people. She looked around the field. A place to escape. A glowing cigarette jumped from mouth to hand as a few of them, black indistinguishable lumps, shifted and studied them.

She could jump in the bushes. She knew enough to dive under the thorns and crawl. Jon would be no help at all, she was sure. Perhaps he even knew them. He said he came out here all the time.

Two young girls. Around ten o'clock. They'll never tell.

Annette had seen them. She waved and said hello.

They were mumbling, but nothing overt. No sudden movements.

The bus, with its eerie greenish interior lights, came almost at once.

"Sure you wouldn't like to stay?" Jon didn't even sound hopeful. She had a vision of them in the bushes. Herself at a respectable distance, pretending not to hear.

On the subway a Spanish-looking man, dressed in white from head to toe, and wearing sunglasses sat opposite Melissa. He was chubby and sweating slightly. She wondered what kind of a so-called man would wear sunglasses at night. Only a very insecure one. Maybe he was blind, sensitive about his weight. Probably a real Mama's boy. Mama shouldn't feed him so well.

Tilting his sunglasses down, he looked right at her and began fondling his crotch.

Annette hooted and dug Jon in the ribs. "Hey!" she pointed. "Check out Romeo!"

Melissa laughed out loud as Romeo jumped up quickly and made for the far door. He got off at the next stop.

Jon glared at them.

"Did you have to make a spectacle of it?" He hissed. Feeling that they did not understand, he emphasized each word as if talking to young and slightly stupid children. "The whole train saw."

"Good, I hope he's absolutely mortified." said Melissa. The other passengers were grinning.

"Well, I don't know what you have against men," said Jon grumpily.

For Annette's sake Melissa kept quiet, but they caught each other's eye.

"If you ask me it's all a myth."

"What is?"

"The insatiable sexual desire of the American Male."

Jon picked up an abandoned POST and began flipping though it ostentatiously.

At a downtown stop a perky and somewhat chubby blonde got on. Her hair was permed into frizzled curls, her nails carefully painted a brilliant orange. She knew Jon and after a hard, knowing glance, summed up Annette's long tanned legs and high cheekbones as not really his type. She talked animatedly with Jon all the way to his stop, ignoring Annette and Melissa completely after the first incredulous "Oh, you're together?"

They got off at the same stop. She was six inches shorter than Jon, Melissa noticed. Subordinate, if you didn't count weight. He gave them a pathetically triumphant smile as he exited. For a moment he looked just like Romeo.

They got back to the apartment around midnight.

"Well, he was nice, I guess," said Annette. "We should have gone on a weekend. I think he was tired. He never tried to grab me."

"He asked me to a movie while you were changing." said Melissa.

"Him too?" Annette sounded resigned. "Why doesn't anyone scheme to get me? I look too boyish, I guess."

"He was just trying his luck. You know how men are."

"I'll end up a lonely old lady." said Annette.

"Not you."

Across the courtyard the lights were out, but here the kitchen was warm and bright.

Not me. Not you.

The Last Hotel

Juliette, after a year in Europe, had met them all. Students, young, talented and handsome, who had no money and asked for loans. And asked for them arrogantly, as if it were their due. Godlike Swedes, with the minds of little children. Paunchy married men, expecting something for very little indeed. Elderly gentlemen with lineages on trains who, recognizing the look in her eyes, invited her for supper. They often had money, but never really enough to make up for themselves.

All of them neatly dressed, hair nicely trimmed, looking prettier than she did half the time, knowing. Knowing where they were going, sure of why they were doing it, certain it was the right thing.

Juliette was not sure. She was not certain. She even let herself appear naive, thinking that she might be more alluring then. But that worked only for very pretty, young, fresh girls. What she had hoped to find had not appeared, She wanted a niche, a place, a possession of her being by a spirit of knowledge. She wanted to know what to do. She wanted it to be easy for her, just like it was for everybody else.

She had been smart enough to go to Europe for a year, when she got the insurance money from her bike accident. She had never been overseas, but she suddenly realized things would never be right at home. Expectations were too high and she was too easily placed. Unmarried, a little chubby, of no consequence. For a moment she had thought of college, but it was a lot of work and she had never done well in school. Even if she succeeded, where would she be? Back home, Sarasota, Florida had no path for her to take. And she wasn't pretty or smart enough to go and win over a city like LA or New York.

Who could she be? What would suit her? What part could she believably play?

A quiet pale music teacher, perhaps. Talented and mysterious. Unleashing the hidden talents of her proteges. But honestly, in spite of years of piano lessons, she had no talent. How could you unleash talent if you didn't have any?

The cruel mistress of a famous man. A continual reminder that he was not as all-important as his sycophants encouraged him to believe. But she didn't know anyone remotely famous. She had had only two boyfriends in her twenty-four years before Europe and she had had to pursue both of them.

A painter, whose works miraculously restored the hopes of thousands with their clarity, pure spirit, and simplicity. She was studying painting, but no brilliant inspirations had occurred yet.

A mysterious recluse, in a little apartment on the Blvd. St Germaine. Not beautiful, but compelling. And whenever you needed advice, she would be the perfect confidant, with the answers to all your difficulties. Apartments on St. Germaine are high, however. Somehow you had to get there before you could be wise and helpful.

And no waitress, however beautiful, is mysterious. A certain note of understood commercialism began to creep into her dealings with men.

At one time she had pondered how best to help humanity. Minister the sick? Train the poor? But the poor and sick were always surly. And perhaps she was one of them, anyway.

Now and then she took time out from her occasional art classes to work. Her money was beginning to dwindle—the end was in sight without the hoped-for outcome.

She worked as a clerk in a souvenir shop or sometimes as a waitress. Her art studies required her work not to be absorbing, so she could devote her mind to things of greater importance. She gave English lessons sometimes, but those jobs never lasted.

Somehow the kind of work she did never paid much. She had to work longer than she would have liked to get even that. It was hardly worth it, she realized dimly. Somehow work had crept up on her and was all she ever did or would ever do.

On the summer beaches she tried to reach a conclusion, but nothing came. She and a chance companion, a Greek, with snake-braided hair, would come close, touch an eternal flame, look closely into each other's eyes for a week of nights. Then he would be gone. Her heart would ache at the transience of all things human. After a while her heart did not ache and she noted a certain glibness and tolerance in their eyes as they mouthed the expected phrases. Events began to have a certain predictability.

It was time for something to happen to her.

Then, at last, her dark hair and pale face attracted a man. A boy really, pale and dark also, so they might have been brother and sister. On the beach he smiled charmingly and removed his glasses the better to charm. He was thin and his eyes a weak blue, but that was all right, The handsome ones thought they didn't have to do anything else but offer their beauty to someone. This boy was unassuming at least, without being too eager to please.

"We have met surely, at a party last year. With your husband. No? No husband. What a pity. For him. You are not French? It is not your accent, but that mysterious smile. So sad. So reserved." His glance took in the sandy beach, filled with youth, not at all reserved.

She was older now, than most of them. Though surely not too old. Not ridiculous yet. Old enough to have character. She was lazy, that was her main flaw. The energetic attract like candles, even when they had no beauty or money. But she was always tired now. Life was wearing her thin.

She was ready for anything. She would do anything. Join a gang of bank robbers. Have a flirtation with a successful drug smuggler. She had had a close brush with the white-slave trade, and only throwing up suddenly and disgustingly in a dingy bar had saved her. No one ever offered her a small part in a quasi-respectable art film, but she suspected there would be no glamour to it in the end.

She knew girls who had, or said they had. Drugs had entertained her for a month or two…Unfortunately her nose bled at inopportune moments and her user boyfriend had no more idea what to do with her than she did.

*   *   *   *

Justin asked her to a discotheque that night and she accepted. After all, if she would consider a dangerous drug smuggler, why not a weak-eyed poet? If that was what he was. He might have friends, also. Somebody interesting.

The disco was a dark hole, filled with dangerous-looking types who did not dress well. Justin allowed melancholy to play over his features as he spoke of Tiziana, a cruel creature who had toyed with him. "But not so pretty as you," he added helpfully, but maybe a little too patly.

She knew she was pretty again in the red-tinged light. It gave a glow to her features and smoothed out the rough edges time had left on her mouth and skin.

Her parents were dead, she told him, and there was a little insurance money left, not really enough to get by on and dwindling fast.

His family owned a hotel on the coast. He was an only child and lived at home still.

At one time that would have been reason enough to drop him. To allow her eyes to wander to the dance floor, to leave him with the address of last month's pensione. Instead her mind racked up the receipts of a thirty-room hotel, the clientele of the coast, the nearby clubs, the beaches and bars. He was, after all, an only child and would inherit it all. She had always loved hotels, to live in one would be wonderful and comfortable. She liked comfort better now, after trudging downstairs for a shower every other night, and across the hall for the toilet. Cracked plaster was not as romantic when the rooms were dark and small and had no TV. The rooms of life had dirt in the corners, now.

He listened to her attentively, as she explained she studied art (but not for a while now), while pondering the essential aloneness of the human condition. He held her hand tenderly and gazed wearily at the crowded, frenetic room. "Such children."

At once she realized she had nothing whatsoever in common with this man. He was waiting for her to coddle him, to minister to him, to uncover the dark genius inside. All this she saw in a blinding flash, because it was what she wanted from him. He had no blinding flash of his own. She realized this was because her wants had never troubled his mind to begin with.

To be admired and petted. It could work out to her advantage. If he did not guess her needs it would not worry him that he could never satisfy them and therefore, someone else might be expected to.

For now, she would settle for him.

*   *   *   *

She was quite clear-eyed about the matter, no romantic illusions were left. And she would not be disillusioned later to discover his legs were scrawny, his mind limited in fatal ways, his perception of her personality narrow and constricting. He might never know her depths, might never guess at them.

She constructed an attitude for herself "—he was so kind, when others weren't—" a quiet sad smile. Her thinness bespeaking a hard past. "—If not for him I could have starved. I owe him everything—"

And the burning look in reply. "My darling, gratitude is not passion."

She would do her duty gracefully, as if she never guessed there might be joy she deserved. In a hotel, surely someone would come her way, someone would stop in the bar while she was serving perhaps, an editor would pick up some scrap of poetry, a photographer would see in her face a mysterious wisdom. A group of young artists would gather to talk and drink. There would, of course, be beefy married business-men determined to squeeze the last drop of excitement from their trips. Elderly couples in retirement, rich old ladies gabbling on and on about their faded pasts. But somewhere, was what she yearned for. She had only to keep waiting.

Justin watched her, perhaps determining to settle in his fashion. Wanting someone with more money, more chic, tidier hair and more admiration for him. He would learn, in time, her magical qualities and finally, when she left him, settle for some plumpish, local girl. But always remember her luminosity. They would remain friends, wist-fully. The little wife resentful, but no competition.

*   *   *   *

Juliette would be the perfect wife for Justin, his parents agreed. She came from Florida, or Oklahoma or some American place far away. Justin needed a wife who would not be a bother to him. He was deli-cate and melancholy and she should understand. She was quiet and would, in time, know him better. It only needed training.

The hotel was off season. The hottest summer weeks were upon them. A few elderly couples among the wilting palms in the lobby and two young men, more than friends, who neglected to pay their bill.

Their apartments were on the ground floor, with the public rooms, the dining room, now closed, the bar, always open, and the lobby, with its yellow lamps.

It was not a great hotel or even a fine one, but that was more than Juliette had hoped for. It was not cheap either, and was quite near the sea. The entertainments were lackluster off-season. Never was there any cultural life.

One night they had eaten dinner in the parents' rooms. Juliette had a room upstairs, gratis, where Justin spent most of his nights. It was evening, for they ate late, and Justin's father was smoking. He was a man of middle height, white-haired and almost distinguished, but you could not help noticing a certain hardness and a coarse laugh. His wife was scrawny and harsh-featured. They both seemed capable of living forever. They rarely smiled. Mr. Brandeis's cheerful air was brutally insistent. Mrs. Brandeis served them. At least she served her son and husband and did not mind Juliette.

They had cognac after dinner as Madame Brandeis cleared the table behind them with muted clinks. She had been a hotel maid before her marriage, she informed Juliette, a very good one.

Juliette sat under a yellow floor lamp in a decrepit upholstered rocking chair. It was the one piece of furniture in the room that was not perfectly clean and neat. They insisted that she sit there for some reason. The garden door was open. The dismal hotel garden of concrete, steel chairs and potted trees. No one was out. It was overcast and damp.

Justin excused himself. Juliette noticed he left by the front door, not going to the bathroom then. Perhaps he had planned a pleasant surprise.

Madame Brandeis looked at her with a little smile. "We're very different from what you're used to, I suppose." She closed the garden door. Was this to be the inquisition? Were they now going to pass their judgement on their son's choice?

Mr. Brandeis stood up. "Well, well. You will be Justin's fourth wife, you know."

"Fourth?" she laughed, not believing.

He sprang forward suddenly and pinned Juliette's wrists. Madame Brandeis dragged back her head by its long dark hair, and chopped off her head with one blow of the kitchen cleaver. She was terribly strong and fast.

The room seemed to whirl as her head dropped, then was caught right side up. Madame wiped her face with a cloth. There were sheets on the floor behind the chair, that she hadn't noticed before. Painter's drops, splattered with red paint.

Mr. Brandeis tipped her body down and caught the blood neatly in a big porcelain soup bowl. He then went to work gutting. Madame tied her head by the hair to a hanging plant as she tidied up the room. The chair was horribly bloodstained. They had bought it at the flea market for this one purpose.

In the midst of this operation came a timid tap on the door. "Are you done?" asked Justin anxiously.

"In a minute dear," said his mother. "Justin is a hundred and twelve, but mentally I'm afraid, about eight. We've trained him though and he does very well. With your help, he'll do perfectly." By now the mess was almost cleaned up.

"Get it well burned, Jules," said Madame, getting out strong twine and a needle. Mr. Brandeis had thrown a cloth over the chair and was dragging it away. There was a glimpse of Justin's worried face in the hall, before the door shut behind him.

Madame Olivia, sewed up Juliette carefully, after packing her with straw. "Don't worry about the scars, dear. It will heal up and barely show." Her body still looked very shrunken. She sewed Juliette's head in place. "You'll need a scarf for a few months, of course."

"It's all right dear," she called to her traitorous son. He slunk in the door, looking oddly eager. "You take her upstairs. It's been quite a shock, I expect."

Juliette tried to speak, but it was now impossible. What had they done? Had there been drugs in the wine? LSD? Was she immortal now? Insane? Should she be grateful or horrified?

"Don't worry about anything." Madame briskly removed her blood-stained apron. "Everything will be simple now."

Juliette wavered on her legs like a stuffed doll. Justin led her upstairs with a tender smile, waiting for her when she tripped and stumbled. He helped her undress and lie down in the cold grey bed. She would have thought it was a dream, except for the horrible stitches around her neck. She felt the edges with her fingers, over and over, as she stared at the ceiling. When Justin left with the clothes she stared in the mirror under the light that seemed so weak. Real. They were real. But they did not hurt.

Justin held her gently in bed that night. The smile on his face reminded her of certain juvenile cousins and their stuffed toys. "Now my darling, I know it's a shock, but it's all over now. Nothing can hurt you any more. You'll keep just as you are, maybe 15 years in this climate. At forty, you'll look twenty-five. All women will envy you."

And no decay into death.

Juliette discovered that she did not sleep. The night was no longer dark to her, but a pale grey shade filled with shapes with no color.

*   *   *   *

She did not eat either, but only took a little wine or hard liquor. The family ate a kidney pie. Whose kidneys? now she wondered. Triumph was in their eyes. Justin's cheeks were flushed and he smiled eagerly in a weak, little-boy way. His parents looked younger, far healthier.

She had thought a weak man would not use her. She had not thought about who was using him. They had gotten to him first. She wondered if he was really their son or just useful window-dressing, bait. They were all dark-haired, but he seemed more delicate than they did.

He took her to the cemetery for a little walk when she became stronger. The stitches in her neck had fused, you couldn't call it healing. There was a scar and she wore scarves and high collars.

He pointed out the graves of his former wives. Died 1912, 1938, 1956. They were buried far apart from each other.

"There was Marie. We had to bury her secretly, since parts were still moving. The method, you see, was not perfected. The rest survived over ten years. Of course, science has advanced a great deal since then. Naturally there was never an autopsy, though we had a close call with Blanche. Luckily the body was quite decomposed when found. The drug is normally a preservative, but exposure to the elements leeches it away."

Juliette spent her nights now in a cold room, hoping it would help. She drank only alcohol and ate only spices, such as the Egyptians used to preserve their dead. She was dead and the dead eat dirt. Or the dirt eats them.

Justin indulged her in this tolerantly, although he told her it would have no effect. "Believe me, my darling, I have done everything possible for you. I don't treat everyone so well. You are very special to me and I couldn't bear to part with you. There are so many young girls who vanish without a trace and no-one cares. Travelers, prostitutes, drug-addicts. Sometimes I think they want to die. They make it so easy. It is only those around them that make it dangerous."

Looking at his pale sensitive face, Juliette could imagine it was. She could imagine him beaten and robbed by an enraged pimp.

"And there are young men too. They are even easier, though not nearly so tender." And he nibbled her ear pleasantly.

*   *   *   *

Among the aged patrons of the bar one evening was a younger man, a German. A bit plump, but well groomed with a fine full beard, fair hair and quiet manners. He smiled at her when she served him and tried four different greetings on her, in Italian, German, English and Spanish. She shook her head.

"What is it? Your boyfriend? Ah, husband. He makes you serve in the bar? Poof, you must leave him. After all, what holds you?"

It was three years now, and she was very tired of her life. She could stand for hours looking out at the rainy garden and plucking at her skirt like a sad crazy woman. The damp was telling on her and she began thinking that Justin's bland reassurances were empty lies. But any other life would weary her too, she thought. There was no heart in her, besides one of baked clay with an image inside it like the Egyptians used to bury in the tomb to serve the dead in afterlife.

Revenge had occurred to her in an abstract way, but she had no enthusiasm for it. What good would it do her? She was not the person she once was and it did not seem possible she would ever be different. No one had saved her at the last minute, The Brandeis' themselves did not know how to restore her.

Now and then she regurgitated in the bathroom and replaced it with fresh stuffing, but the breakdown continued. She was in the wrong climate. Too much rain.

In the cemetery where she and Justin walked the graves were often open. She imagined them, the 19th century victims of a dreadful railway crash, all one family, crawling out into the night. The state of the graves was put down to confusion, a drunken gravedigger or a ghoulish prank. No doubt they had traveled third class, and passed unnoticed in the streets to this very day.

*   *   *   *

They met at the museum in the capital. She liked the place more than any other. The hushed murmurs, the crowds, the many languages, the vast spaces. The paintings, the sculptures of past ages, all done by hands that were deader than hers.

It was autumn, the morning cheerful, but brisk. Geoff wore a cream-colored muffler and his hair was short and blonde above it. They met in a room devoted to the florid Italians of the late 16th century.

He took her out into the gardens.

"Listen, I had a friend with the very same trouble once. It's the breathing. A very simple thing, really. With no air in your lungs there can be no sound. A charming creature you are, so pale, so sad, such dark curly hair. I am a musician. Breath is essential. Try."

She expanded her chest, in the midst of the orange leaves. "Who are you?" Her voice creaked like a coffin lid.

"A simple businessman, with some knowledge of the dark side of human affairs. My brother was one like you. You would last longer in your native soil. You are far from it, I think. Come. We will drink some wine."

The wine bar was small, dark and seedy. Not like the neatly starched corners of the hotel. She felt, not exactly revived, but as if revival were possible. As if this man could save her.

She thought of the unfortunate French queen, Marie-Antoinette. She had her head cut off—had she heard that the body disappeared? Perhaps she had died much later, after scrubbing stone floors for many a long year.

She felt sleepy…A strange feeling. Geoff took her to his room.

They turned down a small alley, then down a smaller, filthier, more deserted one. Then up some ramshackle stairs and through a door into a giant studio.

"My roommate is a artist," he said, speaking quickly, holding her with his eyes. He picked up a knife. "I do the cooking." Without another word he transfixed her to the wall.

"Geoff!" cried a young man. Short and blonde and sensitive. Wearing a soft blue sweater. "What have you done?"

Juliette twitched a little, but she had no strength.

"Look" said Geoff, pulling up her shirt. "No blood. It is not necessary to get them through the heart, or to use a wooden stake."

David crept forward. There was no blood.

"She is one! The walking dead. Pure chance that I saw her."

"Can she see us?"

"As much as she can see anything."

"She is pale, the wine of blood all gone and the heart. But still, the brain, the muscles, the female organs." He shivered delicately, considering. "I wonder, were they saving her for later?"

"How real she looked! Exactly human."

"Don't let it trouble you. She won't be here for long. I"ll take care of it." He embraced David tightly.

*   *   *   *

Shadows crept across the wooden floor. Geoff played Mendolsohn on a small upright piano. David crept in and out, staring at her face. The sound of pots and pans came from the darkened kitchen. She had to keep herself, somehow.

Her hands slipped weakly off the knife. Birds flapped by the skylight, leaving for winter. She forgot what she was doing there.

Suddenly it was dark. The memory of screams occurred to her. Justin stood before her, drawing out the knife. She staggered down the stairs with him.

"You should know better! It was only for your own sake that I asked you not to go out. Do you imagine you are unique? Not at all. A thousand of you in this very city, maybe more. And a thousand of us. They would have destroyed you, you know. All that work for nothing. You are so ungrateful. We have protected and sheltered you. We didn't take everything. Do you think that everyone will treat you so well? You live just as you wanted to. You told me so."

Had she?

"What did they want?"

Justin looked sharply at her. "You talk now?"

"They showed me how. I had forgotten to breathe." She could almost hear him thinking...dangerous.

"They have some knowledge, but are not the chosen ones. They are not of the pure blood and will not benefit as much as we do from human ingestion. Mere butchers. Consider those like you. How convenient for the killer when the corpse gets up, walks away by itself. Is seen in far distant places. Goes about its life for years sometimes, though despondently, and finally dies, a suicide. Why should they look for a missing liver, a few yards of intestine, a missing cripple's limb? The heart is replaced by a cauliflower or a clock. Some twisted boyfriend has kept a corpse for years, dumped it in an alleyway, they died somewhere else. Men who fall under trains and do not die, but walk away, for they were dead already. Predators and prey, who takes notice? The children of men appear in the papers, breed, speak to the neighbors. You are no more visible to them than the birds in the park. Outside the flow of their concerns. Try to tell them you are stuffed with straw. You don't fit in to their conceptions. They would destroy you more thoroughly than even those two."

*   *   *   *

A letter from home came for her. Madame read it carefully. "Your parents have left you a motel in Arizona. Strange. I thought they were already dead."

"The courts take forever." said Juliette. "The wheels of justice, turning." She had summoned the strength to call an old friend and have it sent to her.

"Property overseas." Madame was thoughtful. "What do you think, Jules?"

"Let us go and see."

*   *   *   *

Beside the pool a fat old man in red trunks was contentedly munching the pineapple out of his drink. The hotel was a three-sided building around a pool. It had two stories, iron railings and pink doors. It was right on the highway.

The bottom of the pool was painted a deep peaceful blue. Potted trees concealed the shabby details. The restaurant was small and windowless and not crowded ever. The residents mostly drank.

Dressed in turquoise capris, sunglasses with rhinestones and a scarf, Juliette sat by the pool. There seemed to be something wrong with her eyes. Perhaps she was drugged. She couldn't focus on the details, or make them make sense. Her room number was on her key, 17, or she would have forgotten it. She sat by the pool in the warm dry sun. No one noticed. No one presented her with a bill, or made inquires. It seemed she had some function there.

One evening she opened the windows in her room on the desert side.

The moon was full and the breeze was warm. A grey desert and a greyer ribbon of road across it.

Out on the walkway that ran the length of the second floor she ran into her neighbor. Short-haired and boyish, Maria, the one next door. She was dragging her husband by the foot. A knife was in his chest.

"Give me a hand, will you?" said Maria. "I'm dumping him."

Together they hauled him through the courtyard and across the night highway into the desert. They tumbled him down a little hollow.

"They said I'd get rid of my troubles here," said Maria with satisfaction. "Why are you in the hospital?"

"To lay in my native soil," said Juliette, remembering at last. It was wonderful to be able to help other people, volunteering here at the hospital.

She removed the hay and swallowed warm sand. Bit by bit color returned to the world. She thought of the three bat-winged creatures huddling broken on the shabby counterpane in room 18. A TV buzzed and flickered before their staring eyes.

She smiled. "I should go and collect the rent. It's the only thing that keeps me going, these days."

Immortal Lou

It was when she turned thirty that she first knew. Of course, there was no way she could be sure yet, but still she knew. There are plenty of people who look younger than they are, who at fifty might be forty-two. It was not so remarkable to be thirty and look perhaps twenty-six.

But she knew, just the same. She was the eldest sister, but was often mistaken for the youngest. And she was a full three years older. That was a lot. Her younger sister was married, which made Lou an old maid, but she wasn't teased about it.

Instead her sister would tell her "You're so immature, Lou. Don't you think it's time you settled down? Get a real job? Get married?"

Lou had no desire to do any of it. She hadn't reached the stage where people smiled knowingly at each other in the clubs, over the heads of the other desperate older women. Now it would never happen. There would be other whispers and looks. Jealousy. But why would she need a husband? You only wanted permanence when your body started slowing down. When it felt the chill of the long night approaching, and was afraid to be alone.

There was a trivial quarrel on her birthday. She'd had to work overtime and was late to her own dinner. Her stepmother Karen, who she detested, took it personally. She watched Lou fix herself a drink in the kitchen with a tight smile.

"I suppose you think your little power play worked, leaving us all to wait at your convenience. All that happened was we started without you and had quite a nice time."

"I guess I'll drown my sorrows in drink then." Her father had been hinting lately that perhaps her emotional outbursts were the result of substance abuse. She could guess where he had gotten the idea. Karen was not likely to see the expression of emotion as anything but abnormal. She had personally decorated the tense, all-white apartment with understated furniture of wire and glass. No one stayed long at her parties.

Lou returned to the carefully arranged living room.

"So how does it feel to be thirty?" asked her father jovially.

"Old," she snapped. She didn't feel like discussing it, suddenly. It wasn't really that big of a deal, she thought.

"So tell us, Lou, have you given any thought to what direction your life is going? What you would like to get out of life?" Her stepmother smiled brightly. Any man in your life? was what she meant.

Am I supposed to think that was a friendly question? wondered Lou. "I really wouldn't do anything different. Accounting pays good money and I really enjoy working with the theater group."

"But dear, surely that can't be the sum total of everything, a tiresome job and your little hobby."

This, from a woman whose life consisted principally of shopping.

"The Salk vaccine has been invented already, so I guess the effect I'm going to have on the world is limited."

"It's just that I think, and please don't feel defensive about this, Stan and I know you well and we agree that you're really getting obsessed with this theater thing. Perhaps you're using it as a substitute for real relationships."

"A substitute? That's ridiculous. I enjoy what I'm doing."

"We just want what's best for you, dear."

Her sister spoke up. "You know, the real world is a lot more competitive than Tulsa. A lot of people are just crushed when they get out there and find that out."

"It just doesn't seem worth all the effort you put into it," added her father helpfully.

"What is this, a deprogramming effort?" Lou glared at the three of them. They gazed back with great sympathy. It wasn't that she had any great dreams of being a star, but now she felt compelled to defend herself. Her father and stepmother exchanged a knowing glance. Of course, anything she said would sound desperate and defensive.

The evening was ruined.

"I can't believe you did this!" she said to her stepmother as she stormed out the door. "And on my birthday!"

As she slammed the door she heard her sister say, "Oh Christ, not another scene."

At home she paced around for hours, replaying the evening in her mind. She should have left right at that first power-play remark. She should have known she was being set up. She wasn't being defensive. She had every right to be upset. Why shouldn't she resent them passing judgement on her life? She was basically a happy person. Maybe not a cheerful person, but a happy one. And so what if she got upset sometimes? It wasn't against the law. Did she sneer at her stepmother being kept like a prostitute? At her sister's ignorant husband? It wasn't as if she couldn't.

She stopped and looked in the mirror. So what if she acted like a teenager? She could almost pass for one. Mrs. Perfect Married Andretta couldn't say that. She already had long lines at the corner of her eyes. Having children must do things to you. It could certainly make you fat. Most of the fat women she knew didn't get that way until after their first child. She wasn't fat. Never had been, thank god. She had no desire for children. They made you want them. It was unnatural not to. And if you refused to have any they thought you were getting away with something and punished you for it. She peered closely at her eyes, squinting and turning her head, trying to make them come. Not a sign of a wrinkle. That was exactly what her hair stylist had told her. Of course, he was trying to get a bigger tip. But it was true. No wrinkles.

That jealous old bitch Karen. She knew lots of older women who couldn't stand seeing a young one happy. Wanting her to act like she was an old lady already. What was she supposed to do? Decorate her apartment in beige tones? Date stockbrokers? Get her hair tinted? Sit around at parties in dresses too young for her, passing judgement on younger, prettier women?

Well she didn't feel old, she didn't want to settle down, she didn't like kids and she despised matching furniture.

That's when she knew. So immature. Thinks she's going to live forever. Act your age, Lou.

I'm not getting any older, she realized. Everyone else her age was slowing down, beginning the slow process of decay known as maturity. Of course she seemed mentally young to them. Finding the first wrinkle or feeling the first twinge of arthritis must be like a cancer patient coughing up that first little speck of blood. It would do things to your mind. Probably not good things. Make you bitter and resentful. But with everybody in the same boat, guess who ended up looking abnormal? The one who didn't age.

It would explain so much, her energy, to work late, party later and still have energy for aerobics on her lunch hour. Her disinterest in having children and settling down. Her excitability—so adolescent. Her attachment to her father. Her lack of a serious boyfriend. Everything that seemed so wrong for a thirty year old, was so right for a woman that wasn't half grown up.

She was living at a slower pace than everyone else. And maybe not just slower.

Maybe it had stopped.

"I really don't see what there is to be upset about," said Andretta. "I mean, you make such a big deal out of everything. If theater work is that important to you, go ahead and do it. I just don't see that you've had any big roles, is all." She gave Lou a pointed look.

They were sitting in Andretta's living room, drinking beer. The floor was strewn with books and toys, evidence of her two children. Wondering why Andretta was so negative, Lou remembered telling her once that every woman should at least have a part time job. She hadn't meant to be critical, it was just that she had seen a lot of women who thought they would be supported ending up in minimum wage jobs when they got divorced. It was just self-protection. But maybe her sister had misunderstood. That would explain her hostility. After all, Lou made more money than her husband and he had four people to support. Poor Andretta. How intolerable to think that your own sister was rubbing in her comparative wealth.

No wonder Andretta was always criticizing Lou. She had to feel superior somehow.

Lou resolved to be more considerate. After all how much harder was it going to be when they got older and Andretta realized that Lou was still young?

Her father was seventy-seven when he died. Lou was fifty-seven. At the funeral she told people she was thirty-seven. It was not impossible for him to have a daughter that young. Of course even for thirty-seven she looked pretty good.

An aging woman, one of her dimly remembered aunts, accosted her after the service. "You look good, Lou. I was wondering why we hadn't seen you in so long.

"I'm really busy at work," explained Lou. She avoided the relatives as much as possible. Most of them knew exactly how old she was.

"You don't know who I am, do you?" said her aunt.

She looked hard at the old woman before realizing. "It's you, Andretta." She was shocked. For the first time she felt like crying.

"You haven't changed at all, Lou. The woman sighed. "I suppose if you had some secret process you'd have sold it and be rich by now."

"I really don't know how it happened. You believe me, don't you?"

"Oh yes, dear. You were too young when it all started. So immature. I remember you were the immature one. Never settling down. Not a scientific mind at all. I remember how you always said people thought you were the youngest. I thought you were deluding yourself. I guess you weren't." Andretta wheezed slightly. "How long do you think you'll last?"

"I don't know. Maybe five hundred years."

"You can do a lot in five hundred years." She looked at Lou sharply. "If you last, that is. You could be in trouble, you know, if people ever guess. I imagine the government would be happy to cut you up in little pieces and analyze each one. I don't think anyone would stop them. We'd all like to live forever."

Lou shivered.

"When you have to move on, come and live with me. I'm lonely since Steve died. The children hardly ever visit."

Five years later she moved in and took care of her sister until the day she died. As far as the neighbors were concerned she was Andretta's daughter. She and Andretta grew close, far more so than when they were young.

Near the end Andretta told her, "I've gotten old, and I haven't got long, but at least I haven't been alone. You should get married, Lou. It might ease things a while. I don't want you lonely when I'm gone."

Back in the living room Lou fought back tears and swallowed more beer. Her sister looked at her strangely. "What on earth is the matter, Lou?"

If only she could tell her. Her sister was so young and beautiful now. She had everything and would lose it all, like everyone else in the world.

Everyone but Lou.

"Oh, just daydreaming," said Lou with a weak smile.

She began to view marriage in quite a different light. It was as good a way as any to change your name. A lot of things could be hidden with a new name. After all, she could never apply for social security, no matter how old she got. No one would believe her. She would have to work all her life, moving every decade or so. People could be hateful. Look at her stepmother. Who wouldn't be jealous of a woman who was never going to age? Probably other women would be the worst. Most of them worried constantly about getting old and were quite malicious to the young and attractive, as she had every reason to know.

It would really help to get a husband. It wouldn't matter so much if he were the right one or not. She could always pick up and start over. Her biological clock wasn't ticking, after all.

The problem was finding one. She supposed she could take up some manly occupation like fishing, but just now she didn't feel like the effort. School was another good place, but she'd just gotten out. Maybe later.

In the end she went back to the bars. It was simple, the light was dim, and after a few drinks men found her quite fascinating.

"I'm just in town for the convention," said the man in the suit and, daringly, cowboy boots. "Got an expense account." He flashed a walletful of hundreds at her. "A big expense account."

She smiled her most witless smile. It was strange how you could act totally stupid and no one would guess you weren't. But just try to act intelligent.

"I work for Dynabyte. Big, big company. I'm associate vice president. My card."

"Really? Vice president?" What a jerk. He was the second man in a week to flash his wallet at her. She must look expensive or something. She certainly looked more sophisticated than most of the females in the place. She had on a daring pink leather mini, with a bright fuschia angora sweater and huge crystal earrings. Most of the women in the bar were still stuck at the teased hair and ruffles stage. Of course the older a woman is, the more she knows about clothes. But then, she generally has to.

She watched the VP down his third shot in minutes. He was old. And a drunk. Maybe he had great friends somewhere. Maybe not. It wasn't worth the bother.

"Excuse me, I see an old friend," she slid away painlessly. The VP watched her leave with sadly cynical eyes.

At the other end of the bar a much younger man with a slightly dumb laugh asked her to dance.

He stepped on her toes twice.

"You certainly are a gorgeous lady. You don't mind me telling you that, do you?"

"Not at all." She smiled kindly at him. What a sweet boy.

"You don't seem at all like the other women here. You're kinda sophisticated. I bet you date executives or something."

She sighed.

"You're not married or anything, are you?"

"Me? Certainly not."

"Because if you are, that's alright with me. You look like the kind of chick who might be married to a real rich old fart. I mean, it's understandable. Everybody's got their price."

"I think I'd better run to the restroom."

She scouted the place as she headed to the back. Only two decent guys and they both had dates. Some guy was hanging around the ladies room. Probably Ted Bundy Jr.

"Hey babe, you look real cute."

He had exactly two teeth. She brushed by him.

"What'd I say? Kind of snotty aren't you?"

She was beginning to remember why she had given up on bars. A pity she was stuck at thirty. When you were twenty it was much easier. The men hadn't gotten over their shyness. They were certain they'd do some gauche thing that would be totally unforgivable. By age thirty they didn't worry about doing gauche things any more. They just did them.

"You're so beautiful. I've never met anyone so beautiful."

Lou smiled tolerantly. This guy wasn't so bad, and he seemed shy. She actually had to offer her phone number, he wouldn't ask.

"Do you like oral sex? I only ask because I don't want to lead you on. See it's the only way I can function because my penis is so small and I'm real sensitive about it. I just wanted you to know before things got serious."

Lou wondered how she could get her phone number back.

"Do you want to do some coke? I used to have a bad problem but I can handle it now. Does my hair look OK? I may not be the world's best-looking guy, but I always liked my hair."

"My, it's getting late." Lou stood up.

"I'll call you tomorrow, is that alright?"

She hurried home to unplug the phone.

Maybe once her status became known she would meet a better class of man. Of course, no one would believe her at first. They would give her medical tests that would only prove she was young. So what? There were a lot of young people with fake IDs. They would quiz her on the past. Who had the presidents been? Who won the world series in '87?

Of course she wouldn't know.

They would sneer. "She is clearly the daughter of the woman she claims was her sister. It was not unusual for unwanted children to be raised as siblings. This rather wild tale is a cover for her anxieties regarding the state of affairs."

And she would have to gain wisdom. What with all that time, how could she not be a famous physicist, painter, dancer?

Let's face it. Give a moron a hundred years and he would still never learn to add. She wasn't a moron, but she was definitely average. An average seventy year old was not twice as smart as a thirty-five year old. At a certain point you just stopped learning.

But of course all she had to do was wait. After sixty years of looking thirty they would have to realize she was telling the truth. Maybe then she could make some money. Appear on talk shows. Write a book. If anyone would read it. If they wanted to know what the twentieth century was like there were plenty of old TV shows and movies. It wasn't like the era of the black plague.

And then there were the crazies.

"My daughter has leukemia." The woman looked like she might have it herself. Blonde, pale and bone-thin, her hands trembled ceaselessly. "You have to help us. I know you can. You're two hundred years old. My daughter is only eleven."

Lou shakes her head sadly. She hears stories like this all the time.

"I can't help you. Believe me, I would if I could. Nobody really knows what made me this way. If anyone could figure it out I'd be rich."

"It's not so much. Just one transfusion. You don't know that it wouldn't help. It wouldn't take long. You have forever, after all."

Lou is shaking her head.

"Don't shake your head at me!" screams the woman, clawing in her handbag. "You selfish bitch! My baby is dying! Who do you think you are?" She pulls out a gun and fires repeatedly.

She'd die, of course. She was just eternally young, not a superwoman.

And let's not forget that young people have problems too.

Just that evening, feeling a twinge in her mouth, she looked in the mirror and discovered holes in her teeth. Two tiny brown holes, like termites had been at them. Lots of young people were martyrs to their teeth. After the first set they don't grow back, after all. They didn't heal like scratches did, they just wore gradually away. Perhaps in the end she'd have wrinkles too. Bend an immortal piece of plastic a thousand times and it would show a mark. She would have accidents eventually. Break an arm, a leg. They would heal, but never be the same as before.

And think, in fifteen years she'd bounced checks only once. But at that rate in six hundred years she'd have done it fifty times. Think how that would look on her credit record. And every generation she'd have to go back to college. Not just to catch up. Because who would believe a thirty year old woman with a thirty year old degree?

No wonder she felt so tired. Life was twice as hard for her as everyone else.

She thinks it's been almost forty thousand years. People have changed a lot. She couldn't really call them people any more. The gene pool is much smaller, so many people killed in so many wars. Those that are left have been genetically corrected. Everyone has a seamless, perfect look. She does not resemble them. She is afraid to try correction, it might destroy her immortality.

There are people tailored to living in space, to living in the depths of the sea, to living in the Arctic. Some read minds, or perhaps only subtle scents released by the body. They wrinkle their noses when they meet her, and look puzzled. She gets along by claiming to be a primitive. A purist. Aspects of her presentation are criticized by the experts. They feel there are flaws in her conception of past genotypes. She almost agrees with them.

She keeps a garage in a little ghost town in what used to be Arizona. It is stacked with the memorabilia of her life. Scrapbooks, diaries, clippings of things she doesn't remember doing. Perhaps she didn't do them at all, maybe they were the doings of long-ago friends.

Her diary was many volumes, but she hadn't started it until she was over two hundred. She had written down everything she had remembered of her early years, but who knew what she had forgotten, what was simply wrong?

She still had a photo of her father. Her sister's face had vanished with the centuries. The day she didn't recognize his picture she knew it was time for an end.

She was alone in her garage, under an old incandescent light. Dust rose in soft clouds from the floor. Everything she knew was gone. The world was inconceivable to her. Studies of the past were out of favor. Archaeology was dead. When they found her they would not care.

There is only so much room in the human mind. Now she would have to let go, or die here. She would see only the memory, played again and again before her eyes.

They would sweep away the junk without a glance, perhaps build a bonfire with it. They would dispose of her body swiftly in the flames. Not even an autopsy. Her differences would die, and what humanity once was would disappear forever.

Her stepmother splashed her slightly chubby legs in the shallow end of the pool.

"It's so hard to find a decent job these days. I want something that would truly make use of my qualifications. I would hate to prostitute myself at some horrible little clerk's job, peering at a computer screen all day. Money isn't everything."

"Indeed," remarked Lou dryly. As an accountant, she spent most of her time in front of a computer.

"I don't know how you do it. It would just stunt my soul. I feel there should be a certain grace and harmony to life. A sort of elegance. I need to feel free of everyday sordidness and vulgarity."

"You're so much more sensitive than most people," said Lou, without a trace of sarcasm.

It was easy to be tolerant, when you were never going to die.

Bank of the Damned

As the sun falls a fearsome change overtakes the night workers of the mighty First National.

In the Transit department, dedicated to encoding your checks and speeding them on to their final destination, Michelle Landers at first believed she was imagining it. Imagining the scuttling sounds in the empty hallways, the mysterious thuds and slithers from darkened offices. And in the Trust department, dimly visible through the mandatory glass walls, a large cocoon wreathed in strands of toothpaste green.

Perhaps it was only a large plastic trash bag, probably it didn't really move at all, clutching a tattered shopping bag in one encased paw, as it struggled feebly to be free.

When had it begun?

They had fired Louisa, the old (very old) Transit supervisor, with appalling suddenness. Why, no one knew. True, the woman was incredibly ancient. Her hair was dyed a ghastly orange. She drank. Every lunch in the club on the top of the bank building included two gin and tonics. And certainly she could not cope. But what did this have to do with her job? None of the supervisors could cope and they all drank in the club at noon, sometimes not coming back from lunch at all.

Louisa had left tearfully, decrying the inhuman monsters in the Personnel department.

No-one realized then how true it was.

*   *   *   *

The new supervisor was a zombie named Ronnie Clark. Risen from the grave, one of the undead. Not quite human, not quite an imitation. She kept the air conditioning turned up high no matter what the outside temperature. Naturally. It was necessary to prevent her premature decay.

And the woman never blinked. Ever.

Contact lenses wearers often have the same problem. But even they have eyelids. Not Veronica Clark. She had the lashless eyes of a lizard. The long twitching nose of a depraved coyote. Here and there, the scaly skin of a snake. It was easy to guess that she had met her end in some lonely desert, victim of a serial killer, or a one-car accident, falling asleep at the wheel. Certain parts of her body had been too far gone to be reanimated, so they had been replaced with whatever was handy. Or in some cases, not replaced at all.

And she was not the only one. New beings were quietly taking the place of ordinary Transit workers at First National Bank.

These blank-eyed creatures shuffled closely behind the doomed workers of the department, clumsy, feeble-minded and always willing to lend a hand. At first Michelle had mistaken them for normal trainees, but as one by one her fellow employees were overtaken and replaced by these foul duplicates, these inferior copies, she began to suspect the awful truth.

High turnover, they called it.

The fiends.

*   *   *   *

IMPORTANT!!
SHUT LID BEFORE USING

The sign over the copier was quite clear. You can't say they don't give you a chance, if only for the sport of it.

Michelle was in a hurry that evening. She slapped down the torn check and pressed the COPY button without shutting the lid.

There was a blinding flash of light and when her vision had cleared there was a weak copy of herself standing next to her, grinning vacantly and wobbling in its brilliant blue Japanese thongs. It shuffled after her uncertainly, but doggedly.

To no avail did she glare and make shooing gestures. There was no escape, not even in the bathroom.

*   *   *   *

She could not draw attention to the situation. Those who would care, would not believe her. Those who would believe, would not care. And then they would take steps to silence her, as they had Louisa. With her replacement so close at hand, learning more of her job every day, no-one might even notice she was gone.

Of course anyone could see the insidious cunning of it all.

"Michelle, we have a problem," whispered Ronnie intensely, two inches from Michelle's right ear. Michelle jumped slightly at the sound of her name. Ronnie had a way of sneaking up on a person and informing them of their transgressions as if they were blackmailable offenses.

In just such a way would a seedy little balding man edge up to you on the bus and with a knowing smile say, "I saw you and the dog last night…and I took pictures."

"Come to the manager's desk, please."

Standing in dishonor before the Transit desk, watched by the blank and spiteful eyes of her fellow Transit workers, Michelle looked down into the glazed orbs of the inhuman Veronica.

"You forgot to post the Bankcards yesterday."

Behind her left shoulder (where superstition says Death himself stands, if you look too quickly, so don't) Michelle can just barely see the unfortunate creature Ronnie has singled out. Yes, there is some resemblance, but she is two inches shorter and a good twenty pounds heavier than Michelle.

And her clothes!

"You do know to post the Bankcards?" One thing about these zombies, they are very persistent. "You DO remember?"

To her left the Copy drools and nods and blinks apologetically.

"For your own previous knowledge, Michelle, you have been shown." Ronnie's grasp of English grammer has deteriorated along with her brain. "Isn't that right?" Tap tap tap goes the pen on the open checkbook. Veronica has been figuring her balance. Michelle can read upside down and notices that it is pitifully small, but then zombies have few expenses. Perhaps only…refrigeration. Every night the little light comes on as they crawl into the deep freeze and slam shut the door, like a coffin lid, behind them.

A hint of emotion creeps into the flat opaque eyes of the being before her. Michelle realized that deep thought can pass for sullen silence.

"Is there something you don't understand?"

Interestingly enough, Michelle's major is accounting. The zombie before her, while it yet lived, barely managed to graduate from high school.

"You post it on all the total lines and both our credit and debit lines. This is for conveniently procedural balancing."

Conveniently procedural balancing? A concept of creative banking, no doubt. Dating perhaps from the free-spirited sixties, like Veronica's red-checked bell-bottoms. No doubt they were the current fashion at the time of her demise. They still, ever so faintly, reeked of the grave. Of mold, of poverty, of futility and depression and a lack of fashion sense. How long since bell bottoms were actually worn? For so long that some people are actually wearing them again. But cherry-red and white checked bell-bottoms? Surely never. Perhaps Veronica comes not from the grave, but from a place very much further away, where the stars twinkle brightly in the firmament of the imagination.

Yes indeed, the Twilight Zone.

The zombie is not satisfied. Something in Michelle's attitude is not quite right. An element of nervousness enters into her manner. Is it possible that deep within, the real Veronica Clark has begun to awaken, to realize the full horror of her situation? Barely older than Michelle, she is doomed to crawl across the earth, performing tasks of no significance to anyone, living or dead, for perhaps all eternity, and for barely more than minimum wage.

Veronica leans forward confidingly. None but they will ever learn the full extent of this tragic error. "You know, the whole bank was out of balance last night, by THIRTY THOUSAND DOLLARS. It took them TEN minutes to find it. I'm afraid..." her voice sank to an awful whisper. "I'm afraid that this will go in your file!"

Michelle recoiled in surprise and fear, hastily making the sign of the cross, and the whole enterprise, Veronica, desk and transit department vanished in a puff of smoke and a roar of hellish laughter.

*   *   *   *

Excerpt from the file of Michelle Landers...to make a hand gesture of any kind while being reprimanded by a member of management is a serious offense meriting rebuke.

The tide has washed her up on the dark stony shores of the First National. Outside the stars twinkle brightly over the surf of Friday night traffic, happy yuppies rushing to trendy wine bars in their bright blue BMWs. If she were out there, would the undertow drag her down? Down the asphalt beach, dressed in Salvation Army clothes, stepping over garbage, mumbling to herself as bag ladies do before the tide rushes in and they are drowned, even as Louisa was, not so very long ago?

∗   ∗   ∗   ∗

Michelle's file lay forlornly on the personnel director's desk. Corinne (We are all on a first name basis here at first National. No artificial social boundaries. Only artificial financial boundaries, perhaps.) tapped long, polished and devastatingly false nails across it. Corinne was a suited and possibly bewigged creature, not a single black strand out of place, glued down no doubt, to counteract the effects of Ronnie's weathered sandals and, today, a light polka-dotted sundress through which her beige (or perhaps very dirty) underwear clearly showed. They're ganging up on Michelle. Cutting her out of the herd. Do zombies run in herds? A quagmire of zombies. A cataclysm of zombies.

Tap tap. Yes the file is quite bulky. Every mistake she has made this year is right there in black and white. Only for her benefit. This file will not be used to cut anyone's throat, Michelle. Of course, two novels could be written on the back of these xeroxed sheets. And such mistakes. Her handwriting is sloppy. A three cent error. She abbreviates. Entry not initialed twice. She forgets to sign her complete first name. This could cause her to become confused with all the other M Landers in the bank. Are there other M Landers?

Ah, but perhaps there will be. Some day.

And all of these mistakes so very costly to the bank. She had once dared ask for a dollar and cents figure. This insolence had been noted in her file and she was informed that all mistakes were serious. Very very serious. And not to be tolerated.

Who will take you in, with all these mistakes on your record? Who will give you a job, should we be forced to terminate you? Who will love you? Who will feed you? How will your children survive, when you finally do produce some? You should be grateful. Grateful you even have a job. Some of the girls are so loyal they take their work home with them at night.

A shining example to us all.

Ronnie looks pitying and triumphant at the same time. A hideous expression. They can't mean to erase Michelle yet, surely. How can they replace her? Besides, her copy has not followed her in. It cannot. For she has learned how to repel it utterly.

Magical clothes.

Clothes worn by magazine people. Uncontaminated by the mummy's hand. New, expensive, never worn before, not even once by your sister.

Now Michelle knows why wages are so low. To keep her from buying these magical clothes.

Michelle's eyes slide over Corinne's desk. A neat workbasket, a gold pen, pictures of two blonde children. Blondness is recessive isn't it? Then Corinne's black hair must be a wig. Power hairdressing. She strived to pay attention and not appear distracted.

"—public incident. Veronica is your supervisor, you know. You must show her all due respect. She is your superior."

No one who wears a polyester sundress ten years old that you can see right through is my superior. But perhaps that is unfair. She has children to support after all. It is wrong to judge people by the way they look. Even if they look like plastic dolls, Corinne.

"I won't be insulted, Michelle. I just won't put up with it." Ronnie sounds a little anxious.

Corinne's eyes glow like mirrors. There are no depths there. She is watching Michelle for any change of expression. For a clue to what's really going on. Something she will single-handedly discover, that will make the situation transparent and all Michelle's fault. She will send them back to the Transit department, marvelling at her deep perception.

Veronica is carefully justifying her position. Her lank hair falls loose around her shoulders. Dead hair doesn't curl. Her eyes are glassy. Perhaps they are glass. Pecked out by vultures and later replaced. No need to blink if your eyes are glass.

"Perhaps you feel the job is beneath you?" insisted Ronnie. "A college education means nothing, you know. It has no relevance to the job. We must all work together somehow. You either fit in or you don't."

Means nothing? Ah, the envy of the damned, who are of course refused admission to any school, even junior college.

"You're the same as anyone else in the department, Michelle. You're not paid to have opinions, you are paid to obey. You are all equal in my eyes."

Yours and God's, eh?

"You will follow the pacific rules we have laid down. You will obey standard procedures, even if yours seem more efficient. To you."

Yes, we are all the same now. For equality begins in the grave.

Ronnie falters in the midst of her speech. Under-rehearsed, probably. Lost her place. Hopefully she had notes and would not have to start again form the beginning.

"Do go on," urged Michelle politely.

Corinne's eyes bounced back and forth between them. She shifted in her chair and cleared her throat loudly.

"Michelle, it is our hope that you will come to understand your position in li—in the bank. You need a clearer understanding of the policies and procedures of the Transit Department. That is why we are issuing this reprimand. It is our final warning."

"We think your ego may be getting in the way."

Ego. Was that the new buzzword for soul? She was reflected in Veronica's fish eyes, a thousand times smaller than life.

Outside the window, a shadow blocked the sun. Something fell by, trailing strands of toothpaste green, shouting hoarsely. From the sixth floor it was certain death.

Michelle gasped. Corinne and Ronnie looked at her brightly. They had seen nothing. Clearly they thought her close to tears. She opened her mouth.

"We're not here to argue." said Corinne firmly.

On the desk is a heavy bronze nameplate. Corrine Forrest. All management has this sign of rank. With one hand, a title. With the other, a weapon to crack a skull with. Are they trying to send a message from beyond the grave? Release...us...wooo...releeaasssse ussss...from our torment...

Feeling herself losing control, Michelle dug out a kleenex. She buried her face in it and made smothered noises, trying not to laugh out loud.

"We hope you will consider seriously what we have discussed here," said Corinne. "We will support any decision Veronica may choose to make. Even...termination."

The death penalty seemed unduly severe. "You mean I'll be fired?" Michelle managed to ask.

"I'm afraid so," said Ronnie, her face glowing with satisfaction.

A withered hand was scraping at the window. How could they not see?

"We'll let you take a little break dear, before going back to work," said Corinne gently. But firmly. Quite sure that control was re-established.

Muffled in folds of kleenex, Michelle rushed from the room. In the back office she scanned the roof below. No dead bodies, no curious bystanders, no old woman in a toothpaste green nightie. Was it all some kind of vision?

Soon, night will come again.

*   *   *   *

Marshalled into a double row, Copies back, real people front, the Transit workers were sternly lectured.

This was not unusual. Once a week they were subjected to it. Poor idiots, they couldn't stay out of trouble even that long. They were forever coming in late, overstaying their breaks, looking in their supervisors's desk for pens or papers, talking instead of working, and committing a host of other serious violations of bank policy. They could not be trusted to do even the simplest task without close supervision and a show of hostility.

"Each person shall do their own job and nothing else. This job will be assigned by the supervisor. You will not question these assignments. Schedules will be drawn up. Deadlines will be met. Note will be taken of those who fail. Pins will be skewered. Dolls roasted. Any lapses will be noted in your file. Is this clear?"

Shuffling of feet and shifting of eyes. Each one wondering, What brought this on? Was it me? Do they think it was me? There. She glared right at me. I knew it. Well, it wasn't me. I bet it was Susan. Or Michelle. They had her in Personnel earlier. Do they know how she talks about the Holy Bank? I bet they'd like to know.

"Are there any questions?" barked Veronica, in a tone that would immediately discourage any. The workers shook their heads, mumbling, and made tentative motions toward their proof machines. Michelle returned to her desk and began to prepare the day's work to be filmed.

There was a plan. She could sense it dimly. A vast force was quietly being created at the First National Bank. But why? To what purpose? Merely to speed along the checks of people who might well be zombies themselves? What war were they fighting? What was their ultimate aim? What would they do once they had conquered the world? What could they do, being zombies?

"Oh, Michelle," Ronnie was smiling brightly at her.

Michelle paused, the stack of checks poised over the filmer.

"Could you start filming now? Please? For me?"

Michelle looked at the checks in her hand, at the filmer. Was the woman blind? In another space-time continuum altogether? Or—she glanced over her shoulder. Her Copy grinned back. Or talking to someone else entirely? Someone not nearly so bright. Someone who might wear embroidered black open-toed pumps with a khaki split skirt on purpose to work. Instead of by accident. As Michelle had today. She had been in a hurry. She thought they would do. And they would. Almost.

They were taking over her mind.

With a sigh she started filming her work.

As she fed in the checks, she looked over her fellow employees. For a secret army they were sad specimens. Most were chubby, yet still obviously badly nourished, with pale, pasty, acne-prone skin. They all, every last one, had horrible health problems. They discussed these constantly, at great length and in great detail. At least one of them was always in the hospital for a female operation. Or pregnant. Why would women so unhealthy even consider having a baby? Or several babies? On a proof operator's salary, yet. With no husband, unless unemployed or alcoholic. An army of incubators. And they were trying to draft her.

Ronnie is behind her, creeping up silently on large flat feet. If only she would keep her shoes on. Or clip those ugly yellow toenails.

"You mustn't force the checks through, dear. It won't take clarity pictures that way."

Clarity pictures. Michelle suppressed a grin. A certain desperation flitted across Ronnie's coyote face, and just as quickly, vanished.

"Be sure to guide them. We wouldn't want a jam."

She smiled brightly at the drooling Copy behind Michelle that cannot even operate a simple film machine.

Research has shown that there are two ways to rid yourself of a zombie. Stab it with cold steel. Yes, a knife through the heart will keep the eternally restless from wandering. Unfortunately it keeps the completely normal from wandering as well. It is difficult to explain that you merely meant to kill a person already dead, with them lying there dead and pale as a fish, reproaching you silently with their staring eyes.

The film machine clattered. Jam. Rumpled checks and bits of checks poured out gracefully over the counter.

Across the room, Ronnie clicked her tongue and shook her lank curls with an exasperated sigh. "Now Michelle, common sense…"

She does know, after all. Yes indeed. How to PREVENT JAMS. Mystical hand gestures. Secret words. Do they work? Just as well as guiding the checks. Just as well as locking yourself in the bathroom and drinking yourself silly. Louisa had done that. The trouble was, no matter what you did, your efforts to escape led you right back to where you began, only worse, the grey empty years stretched out before you, and not even drinking allowed.

Gently, carefully, precisely, Michelle gathered up the checks.

She took her lunch alone, at seven-thirty, to avoid the endless discussions of how many times little Jimmy puked today and what major household appliance he had recently destroyed because his loving zombie mother could not be at home, where she belonged, to guide him. The bank was dark and silent, the cleaning people yet to arrive.

She salted the stale vending-machine potato chips, then stared at the salt shaker. Salt, the second way to kill a zombie. Best to be prepared. She slipped it in her skirt pocket.

The silence waited.

From the Trust Department, the sound of scratching. Scritch scritch. A mouse is trying to escape. Or perhaps it is working late, drawing up a contract. There is a light in the back office. The doors are locked, but there is always a way around. Check dust, like fog, filtering the light between the dim grey rows of desks. The cocoon lies unwreathed in a chair. Whatever it contained is free. Shivering, Michelle passes on.

And there she is, back in the Transit department.

She blinks, momentarily disoriented. There must be a shortcut here.

"—if you ask me, she's on drugs—"

"—I mean if you don't like it here you can always leave—"

"—college kids—"

The snide comments cut off with a few giggles when she appears. There is a smell in the air, as of the grave, or the garbage heap, where the dead rot and the living are…worms. The inhabitants of the garbage heap shoot meaningful looks at each other. Waiting for her to attack or retreat. Waiting for her to give a damn.

It will be a long wait.

*   *   *   *

Like a stage show the lights dimmed. The workers sat silently at their machines, pale flabby statues. It was midnight. Natural law had been suspended.

And outside, a great full moon rose over the Holiday Inn.

The only other light came from the glass-walled office of the imperious Howard, chief of them all. Ronnie was sitting inside at his desk, borrowing grandeur. Someone Michelle knew sat in one of the other chairs. Like Michelle, she wore a khaki-colored skirt, although hers was of some cheap fabric with an uneven hem. Furthermore her hair was unpermed and her blouse had short gathered sleeves. With ruffles.

Michelle stepped into the office. Venetian blinds rattled against glass walls as the door slammed.

The Copy sits mutely, eyes on plastic thongs. Michelle's heart is beating rapidly as Ronnie graciously motions for her to sit. Each Transit worker had faced this moment and failed. Now, tonight, they wanted her soul. And if she refused, it was six stories down.

For there is but one escape from the Bank of the Damned.

Through the blinds, the casual glances of the curious. She clutches the salt shaker in her pocket.

"I want you to read this, Michelle, and then I want you to sign it."

Veronica speaks crisply. She hands Michelle a paper and pen. With a very very sharp point.

"In the appropriate fluid." Veronica smiles with naked hostility. "There will be a change in attitude. A permanent one."

The Copy stares in bewilderment. She doesn't understand. But she will do as she is told.

Michelle reads. "—I will resign my soul to the First National, for all eternity—"

"If not—" Ronnie makes an ambiguous gesture that might, just might, have indicated the window.

There is a fourth person in the room. Silently as a ghost she appears beside Michelle, her nightie flapping like green smoke, her eyes blazing. She died in that nightie, yes she did, a six story plunge. They had read about it in the papers. Proud Louisa, who would not submit.

Her hands reach into Michelle's hands, her feet into Michelle's feet. She stepped into Michelle's body as you would put on a coat.

"I'm possessed," whispers Michelle, amazed.

"What?" says Veronica loudly, hoping yet to gain control. "What did you say, Michelle?" A third eyelid blinks, like a fish.

Smiling, Michelle gently closes the venetian blinds. Out in the department no one noticed anything odd.

"What are you doing Michelle?" asked Ronnie sharply, but it squeaked a little at the end.

So much more effective to say nothing. Michelle stood in front of the door. She had them both trapped.

"They'll be needing me," said Veronica quickly, sensing danger.

"Not for a while," said Michelle, pausing dramatically. "You've seen to that."

Veronica's eyes darted about, seeking escape. Smiling hugely, (and sadistically, Ronnie would later claim) Michelle pulled out the salt shaker and sprinkled it over her Copy's head.

With a horrible burbling cry it dissolved into grey slime and trickled over the carpet, leaving scummy bubbles behind.

"Just like a slug," said Michelle thoughtfully. In her youth she had also incinerated water bugs with sparklers on the Fourth of July.

Ronnie looked as though she might bolt, but it was a long way to the door around the desk and Michelle blocked the way. Michelle threw the salt directly in her face.

They said her shrieks could be heard in the lunchroom.

Unfortunately Michelle's assessment of the situation was a bit off. Perhaps under the zombie lurked part of the living Veronica, unchained and awake at last.

And hysterical.

Howard arrived within twenty minutes. As per usual, the police were not called.

"Now I don't understand quite what went on here—" he said that a lot that night. Some sort of attack had definitely occurred. Or Veronica felt that one had occurred. There was quite a mess on the cheap carpeting. Grey slime. Bubbles. And salt. But still.

"I'm afraid I don't understand."

*   *   *   *

Michelle was fired, of course. Ronnie was, after all, her supervisor. A case could be made for insubordination. That morning she was cast out on the street like a cat choking on a hairball. No job, no references, facing starvation until the unemployment kicked in.

The Zombie's revenge.

Michelle stood outside the doors, drained and despairing. Someone came out of the stairwell and brushed by her with a glance. Susan.

Didn't she use to work here? An old woman came out. Louisa? Could it be?

All with their fingers on their lips. Pointing up silently.

Michelle opened the stairwell door. She stood on the metal steps listening to the faint footfalls disappearing above her.

Then, she followed.

It was many flights to the thirteenth floor. To the club at the top of the building. And in the sharp shadows, as the blazing sun rose over the city, faces she knew. Louisa, Susan, Diane. The dead and presumably living.

The bartender was cleaning up, clinking glasses. It was warm enough up here.

Should she ask? Should she greet them? Should she pretend to know?

Is this it? Did it happen at last? Am I where the bad people go? Is the path to Hell from the Transit department all uphill?

New Year's Eve

New Year's Eve with two twenty-two-year-olds. The more Jeanie thought about it, the more depressing it sounded.

Jeanie was twenty-eight. Not that old, but older. Plenty older. Almost 25% older. Cindi and Lisa were still fresh and pretty. She was slowly desiccating.

Still, none of the three of them had dates on New Year's. Lisa had sort of broken up with her fiance in France (her French romance had been the fascination of everyone at work), Cindi's boyfriend was a bartender and had to work that night, and Jeanie's boyfriend was at home with his mother, who was too ill to see Jeanie.

*   *   *   *

"Let's get all dressed up in our flashiest, sexiest dresses and go out and have a good time anyway," Jeanie had suggested. She was tired of hearing the two of them moan and act miserable all day at the bank.

To her surprise they thought it was a great idea. Almost a startling idea. One that only an older, more sophisticated woman would have thought of.

Cindi and Lisa insisted on going to Blondie's, a popular place that had a much younger crowd than Jeanie would have selected. Who there would appreciate the appeal of their mystery? But Cindi and Lisa were best friends, so Jeanie was overruled. She had known Lisa for years, and helped her land the job at the bank, but Cindi was only an acquaintance. People said she was bitchy, but that usually just meant that a woman was really cute. Jeanie had never had a problem with her.

✳   ✳   ✳   ✳

They met at Cindi's apartment. It was in one of the nicest complexes in Wichita, almost brand new. Every apartment was at least a two bedroom and they all had covered parking.

Jeanie thought her one-bedroom in an old building near downtown had a lot more character. She had decided to wear her blue sequinned mini, shivering in her 35-year-old VW bug all across town. She had made the dress herself to get a perfect fit. She had used a slip of hers as a pattern. It flattered her, hiding her major flaw, a flat chest, and accenting her best feature, her legs. Made to measure clothes always looked subtly better. Lisa showed up in an ultra-tight leather mini and a low-necked red sweater.

Lisa still lived at home with her parents. Her Dad was a criminal attorney and made lots of money off some pretty scummy people. That was how he could afford to send his daughter to France for the summer. But Lisa hadn't picked up any culture there. She had just gone south and spent her days at the beach. She wasn't doing very well in school either. But then she had met Anatole, whose family seemed to own a lot of real estate, so everything was alright. Jeanie now realized she should have gone with her for the summer. But how could she have afforded it? Still, it would have been an investment, three months rent, split with another girl, and you were set up for life. And she just knew she would have met someone a lot more special than that arrogant Anatole.

Cindi answered the door in something ladylike and black and glittery.

"Oooh, that's so pretty."

"I borrowed it from Miss Kansas. It cost six hundred dollars. You know, she's really sweet."

It was a very modest dress, high necked and knee length, covered in beading. Cindi's look at Jeanie suggested she should be feeling a bit naked now. And she should have asked about Miss Kansas and how she was doing. Well, Jeanie didn't care.

"That's a very nice dress too," said Cindi. "Would you like a drink? I need to finish my hair."

"A beer would be nice," said Jeanie.

"There's some in the fridge."

Jeanie helped herself and poured Lisa a glass of wine when she asked for it. The kitchen was of some grim dark wood, but you had to admit it was huge. Something had struck her about her surroundings, but she forgot what it was almost immediately.

"You drive, Cindi," suggested Lisa eagerly. "You've got a nice car. And this is a really nice apartment. Two bedrooms, huh?"

"Yes, two. The rent's pretty high, but at least you get better neighbors. You know what I mean."

No black people.

Jeanie realized she did not have a nice car, or a nice apartment, and it should matter. Why had it taken until age twenty-eight to realize it?

When Cindi was ready, they drove to Blondie's. It was early yet, eight o'clock. Cindi worked there part-time, which was the main reason she had picked it. Besides it would be easier to get in at the last minute on New Year's Eve. She nodded to her friends as they entered. "Wow, you look stunning," said the waitress. "Where're your dates?"

"We'll find some," said Jeanie.

"Mine's in France," said Lisa. "Let's hope he stays there."

Cindi's eyes glittered with ignored, overwhelming emotions. "I have to leave at midnight, you know. I have to go see Johnny at work. I don't want anyone else kissing him."

"Wow," said another waitress. "Don't you guys look great. Where are your dates?"

"Where, indeed. It's probably good Allen isn't here either. He's been a real pest." said Jeanie. "Ever since he asked me to marry him."

"Marry him?"

It was like two rifles pointing at her, the way everyone's heads swung around and their eyes zeroed in at the 'M' word.

"I want to, but not right now. He wants me to move to Oklahoma with him and I just can't see that either."

"And he accepts that?" Cindi sounded a trifle snappy.

Jeanie shrugged. "Does he have a choice? I don't see any need to give up everything for a guy. If he loves me, he shouldn't insist when he sees I'm not ready."

"Anatole keeps asking me to marry him, but I don't know. He hits me sometimes."

"He what?" Now Jeanie swung around. "Forget that. Next time he does it, hit him back with a brick! He's scum. I didn't know he did that. Just dump the jerk."

"Well, it's just slaps, really."

"It's really between the two of you," said Cindi primly. "I don't think you should interfere in another relationship just because you're not happy in yours, Jeanie."

"Who said I wasn't happy?"

"Have you made any resolutions?" said Lisa hurriedly.

"Oh," said Jeanie, "Publish some stories, move the heck out of this boring town. Soon. Before it's too late."

"Finish school," said Lisa, "Move out of my parents' house, get my own place."

"I haven't really thought about it. Finish school, I guess," said Cindi. "Get married, if that's not too typical for you."

"Who's that guy?" An old guy wearing a flat cloth hat had come in and was staring at them. Well, not that old, Jeanie reminded herself.

Maybe about ten years older than her, but way older than the rest of the crowd.

He came over and said hi to Cindi. Jeanie ignored him and swallowed her beer. It figured Cindi knew him. She seemed impressed by the man of the world act, but Jeanie had seen it all before. If he was so great why was he still an unknown on the circuit at the age of forty plus? Apparently he was a comedian, doing a show at the club next door. His name was Alan. Another younger guy joined him, another comedian, this one from Chicago. The old guy was from LA. Wow. Town of meaningless relationships and plastic people. What a recommendation.

"Want to join us over at the club? I think there might be a table free. We can bring guests."

What the heck, it was something new to do. They scurried through the cold winter wind. "Damn, why did I leave my coat in your car?"

"We thought we'd be more impressive without them."

There was a table at the club, and drinks. "Hi, Cindi," said their waitress. Did she know every bar waitress in town? "You guys look really great tonight, like a real New Year's. Lots of people don't dress up any more. I think it's boring." Looking around, Jeanie saw this was true. Most of the women were into Midwest chic, fancy sequinned sweaters, or the business suits they wore to interviews. Be tacky or be dull, those were your choices.

"I'm so fat compared to you guys," sighed Cindi.

"Don't be like that," said Jeanie impatiently. "You know you're not remotely fat."

"So, where are you going after this?" Ancient Alan asked Jeanie.

"I've got bad news for you, buddy," she told him, "In this town all the bars close at 2:00 AM."

"Well maybe we could go to my hotel."

"Yes, Mr. Son of Sam."

Cindi was looking at them fixedly, with a strange expression of pain. "I really have to go to The Fireside. Johnny has to work tonight and I don't want someone else kissing him at midnight."

"Hey, you drove!"

"And you have our coats!"

"Don't worry, I'll be back right after midnight."

*   *   *   *

The show was OK. Jeanie was glad Cindi hadn't stayed to glare and pout. Alan turned out to be bald under his hat and only knew jokes about faggots. Jeanie wished she'd gotten her coat from Cindi. It was cold. It was almost one o'clock and she hadn't turned back up. Jeanie didn't have the twenty dollars for a cab ride. She was stuck.

As Jeanie watched the show, a mental snapshot suddenly developed. What had she expected? When she'd opened Cindi's refrigerator there was only a jug of wine and a case of beer and a dried up head of lettuce. She was living on alcohol.

*   *   *   *

"I really don't drink much," Jeanie announced, after the old guy tried to get her to drink something stronger than water for the tenth time. "More than two drinks and I get a hangover." "Jesus, I'm cold," she remarked to Lisa. Lisa had just run into an old friend. Young, but very cute. "He's like a brother," Lisa said, kissing him in a very unsisterly fashion. "Here, Rick, loan her your jacket. Rick used to live next door to us, years ago. I always said I would grow up and marry him."

"But instead you got some French guy and broke my heart." Rick looked quite used to being teased by women this way.

Jeanie found herself very tired. Age. She used to stay up until four in the morning and be ready to work at seven-thirty.

Well, those days were over.

"Having a good time?" asked Rick. He was perfect-looking, medium-sized with brown hair and long dark eyelashes around his shy blue eyes.

"Oh, time for me to go to bed."

"I feel sorry for you if you do get married," said Lisa suddenly. "You're never happy."

Well, what brought that on? "Happiness is overrated." She said. "I'd rather be self-reliant."

"You know nothing about marriage."

"Marriage is sharing," said Rick. He didn't seem put out by Lisa's snappy tone. Probably she set people straight all the time, and was admired for her honesty.

Jeanie smiled. "How many times have you been married?"

"Once."

"And how many times divorced?"

"Once."

She shrugged. Point made.

"What a nice dress." Interupted Alan, returning pointedly to their table.

"Thanks, I made it myself."

"Wow, you sewed on all those sequins? How long did that take?"

Jeanie burst into loud laughter. The old guy looked hurt. Lisa looked at her like she'd lost her mind.

"Sorry, it was just the thought of all that work. You buy the material pre-sequinned, it's really not that hard." Total silence greeted her. "Well, I'm ready to go."

"I could drive you home," offered Rick eagerly. What was this? Did she feel in a cradle-robbing mood? But her coat, what a hassle to drive across town the next morning. At that moment she saw Cindi across the room. Staggering drunk. Well, big surprise. At least the car was only two blocks away. She could walk if she had to.

Lisa was still talking with Rick.

"Have a good time?" asked Jeanie.

"Not really." Cindi looked pissed.

"So what happened?"

Her mouth turned down. It was a hard little mouth. "Oh, some guys I knew showed up. I hugged them all for New Year's. So what's the big deal? Johnny is so insecure."

"What's going on?" asked Lisa. "You're late."

"It's all over with," said Jeanie. "Johnny's a jerk."

Cindi glared. "No, it's not over with. I don't know why you said that."

"He's too young anyway," said Lisa.

"Twenty-one," said Cindi. "I'm only twenty-two."

"Almost twenty-three," reminded Jeanie. "Forget him, anyway. Men are no good until they're at least thirty-three and divorced once. Don't let him jerk you around."

"Let's go, we've been waiting," said Lisa.

"Well, I don't understand. Did you pay for anything?"

"What?"

"Did you pay for any of your drinks?"

"What drinks? I've been drinking water for the last hour and a half."

"Did you even say thank you?"

"Why should I?"

"At least I know how to behave." Cindi stumbled off to the old man, threw her arms around his neck and practically stuck her tongue down his throat. Lisa and Jeanie watched in astonishment. They were almost the last ones in the place.

"This is stupid," said Lisa. "She doesn't realize the party's over."

"I'm really worried about Cindi," said her little waitress friend. She couldn't have been over 21 herself.

"That's very commendable," said Jeanie, "But do you think you're doing her any favors by paying attention to her when she's like this?" The little waitress looked confused.

"But I'm her friend!"

"Let's go," Lisa said.

"I'll walk you out," said Alan. Rick had magically disappeared. When had that happened? "Are you going to another party?" he asked Jeanie. Cindi had her arm around him.

"I'm an old lady, I'm going home."

"This is my last night in town."

"Lucky you."

Cindi continued talking to him. "Do you play a lot of clubs in LA? Did you ever work with anyone famous?"

"Let's go," said Lisa finally. She pried Cindi free of the old guy and they drove off in silence.

"Well, you two can be stuck-up bitches if you like. A lady should express her gratitude."

"A tongue kiss for a two-dollar drink is gratitude?"

"You could have left any time."

"You drove, remember?"

"Well, who asked me to?"

They were in the parking lot now.

"Don't worry, Cindi, we won't be making that mistake again," snapped Jeanie. To think the whole evening had been her idea.

"Just because you drive ugly pieces of shit. You're jealous and unhappy. I bet that Allen of yours can't stand your ugly face."

"Well, at least a cheap drunken slut doesn't drive our ugly pieces of shit," said Jeanie with great calm. She jumped out of the car. "Happy New Year, Bitchy."

She marched off to her little VW, clutching her coat around her. She had just known something like this would happen. Twenty-two was still so immature.

That would teach her to run around with kids.

PAUL'S WIFE

And Tina's life was fixed, just like that. Everything fell into place and all she had to do was arrange the details.

Falling in love is instantaneous. One moment you are here, lost and alone. The next moment, there. Assured and confident.

When Tina flipped back her calendar from the ballet performance she saw it had only been a week. There, just the Saturday before, she and vivacious little Serena had gone to a trendy bar in downtown Tulsa.

"Poor Paul is so lonely," Serena said. "He doesn't know anyone in town, you know. He just about went crazy over Christmas. He was away from his wife for two months. He invited me to play in his hot tub."

They laughed together knowingly over that. Paul was the principal dancer for the amateur Tulsa company, imported twice a year from a professional company in Denver to dance their leading roles.

"Married men," said Tina. "They're all alike. I was convinced he was gay. Most of the dancers are."

"Oh no," said Serena. "He's been married two years. You should meet his wife. She's older than him. A lot older. She's a nurse. Can you believe it? It's really weird."

"Poor guy," said Tina. "He must have been lonely to settle for her."

＊   ＊   ＊   ＊

Later she wondered about all that detail. Had Paul sent Serena to feel out the situation? But no, it was impossible. When you're in love the smallest sign becomes an open invitation. Hope was to be found in a simple 'hello'. Wishful thinking. She wasn't going to make that mistake.

Paul did not have a ballet dancer's body, long and sculpted. He was short and stocky, almost fat. Extremely muscular, he was closer to a body builder than a dancer. It helped in leaps and lifts, and of course, for a man, there are always jobs in dance. Girls had to be stick-thin, turn quadruple pirouettes and have leg extensions over their heads. It wasn't fair. Tina could never be a professional, not with standards like that. Still, she had some talent and a certain wistful, yearning quality to her dancing.

Paul gave master classes to the troupe. Tina hated master classes, they were too difficult and her balletic deficiencies were commented on, or even worse, scornfully ignored.

Paul gave a rather disjointed class, and she guessed he was not used to teaching back home. But the very last exercise, port de bras to finish the class, was beautiful. She tried not to smile as she watched him wave his arms gracefully and admire himself in the mirror. There was clearly a very feminine side to Paul. It was strange to see it in that masculine body. She didn't imagine that anyone had ever teased him much about it, though. He was very strong. He lifted Serena effortlessly in their pas des deux. True, she wasn't very big, but even a hundred pounds is a lot when you're tossing it over your head with one hand.

Paul seemed happy with himself, without being self-satisfied. Although he was five years older than Tina, he seemed younger. He had a little bit of a frown, but it was a frown of near-sighted concentration. When he lectured the young fencers of Romeo and Juliet about horseplay with their swords his voice was high and a little worried. He had a small speech impediment, you couldn't call it a lisp.

In rehearsal Tina tried hard not to be afraid. She hated performing, but she thought about Paul. It was working, too. She just wiped everything from her mind and pretended. She was Rosaline, out for her morning stroll. Just happened to be carrying a rose. Romeo accosts her, playing his lute. A lover, not a fighter, the perfect part for Paul. She was aloof. But before her exit she turned and smiled at Romeo and tossed him the rose. Or in this case, a plastic lily, the only fake flower they had on hand, left over from Giselle.

It fell to the floor with a deathly plastic rattle. The artistic director snickered. "We'll get a decent flower. And Tina, when you call your guards you're not the kitchen wench calling home the cows. Merely lift a finger. Again. Paul, a little quicker please. Get off the stage before the peasants appear. They'll run you right over, you don't know these awful girls."

They ran through it again. She tried to smile speculatively at Paul as he strummed an imaginary lute and caressed her with his doglike eyes. He really threw himself into the part, even in rehearsal. Reggie, the other professional who was playing Mercutio, did not. Serena had remarked that Paul was a ham. "He just loves attention." It made it easier for Tina, though. She felt that things were going right. He really meant it. It wasn't just acting. Step by step, her new life was taking shape.

In the ballroom scene he flirted with her until the moment he saw Juliet. There was a part where he seized her hand unexpectedly and they danced a slow pavane. She was supposed to look at him wonderingly. As she was about to slip away at the end of the dance he drew her back and mimed passionate infatuation, seizing her hand and pressing it to his heart. Suddenly she felt herself blushing and laughed to hide her confusion. It was exactly what she had wanted to happen. But she hadn't thought how to respond. What did haughty aristocrats do? She couldn't imagine. Paul looked slightly hurt.

"You did that so well," she said, blushing. "I can't keep a straight face. It's so hard for me on stage."

"Here, I'll think of something," he said kindly. "I'll whisper in your ear." He brushed back her hair and mimed an indecent suggestion. She had to tilt her head to make it feasible, she was nearly six feet tall. He drew both her hands into his and adored her with his eyes.

She could hardly breathe. Was it time to make her move?

No, no, not yet.

*   *   *   *

It was a Friday night and she was going out. She changed in the dressing room as rehearsal continued. One of the younger girls came in and stared. "Why Tina, you're so tall and elegant. I've never seen you in normal clothes. You look just like a model."

She laughed self-consciously. "It's all in the tailoring."

She watched the rest of rehearsal for a little bit.

"Going out, Rosaline?" teased Reg.

"I thought I'd lounge around the house, actually."

The artistic director glanced her way speculatively. Tina looked a lot different with makeup on.

She had just turned twenty-six and was still single. Over the quarter century mark. It had made her desperate for a while. A man had actually asked her "What? You haven't even been married once? Doesn't it make you feel uncomfortable to be the only single woman here?" And three times in the bar she had been looked at searchingly and asked, "How old are you anyway?"

She could look at it positively, and think they were wondering how such poise and wisdom could be coming from such a young girl. Actually though, they probably couldn't believe such girlish behavior in a middle-aged woman. Kittenish. She had met kittenish fifty-year olds. Kittenish overweight fifty-year olds. A sight horrible to behold.

Her shyness was half put on, any more. You had to work less socially if you were timid, although she'd never been easy around people. But she wasn't really shy, or filled with self-doubts. Not unless she felt inferior and that rarely happened. She had a college degree, a decent job, and was reasonably thin, why shouldn't she be confident? Maybe she was sending out all the wrong signals, with this timidity.

A week to fall in love. Another week to take action. Still, if she'd been really quick she would have made a move. Or let him make one. Why hadn't she taken herself seriously? She could have wandered off innocently to a deserted part of the auditorium, given him an opportunity, even under the eyes of his wife.

She'd come to the final rehearsals and babysat him with her wretched child. Tina had been surprised to learn of the little girl, then not so surprised. Obviously that was how the lumpy wife had snared him. Poor little thing, she looked just like Paul. She was very rambunctious, but you could bet with her disapproving mother, that she wouldn't be for long.

Sometimes she thought she'd tell someone, Serena, Reg, anyone. But he was a married man. She'd sworn she'd never be such a fool as to fall for a married man. It was as good as announcing you were second best. She had too much self-respect. She'd never let a man have the upper hand like that.

If only she could have slept with him. It probably would have got him right out of her system. Most men were really boring in bed. They hadn't a clue. Sometimes she thought she was more like a man than men were. Love was all very good and well, but he'd better have a decent job and not be too dependant. God knows it should have been easy enough. Hadn't Serena said he was lonely?

She made a list to keep it all straight in her mind. Minus and plus. Minus, he had a child. Plus, he was a loving father. Minus, he was married. Plus, his wife was old, bad tempered and dumpy. Minus, what kind of guy would be attracted to that? Did he have disgusting bed habits? Suck at those pendulous breasts all night? Well, that was a plus, really. She could put him out of her mind if it were true.

He had been extremely kind about her stage fright. That was hopeful. But no, he was a teacher and was merely doing his professional duty. He hadn't pursued her. Maybe he was shy around women. No wonder an older predatory female had had her way with him. At least he didn't care for twittering little girls. But she had acted like a twittering little girl. She hadn't been able to look at him in class, when he'd stood by her at the barre. Naturally he thought she was unfriendly. She hadn't played with his dear little girl, the very image of her father, who you could just bet his wife was holding like a hammer over his head. The little girl wasn't really the impediment though. It was the wife.

He went back home at the end of the season. She found an old program with his picture to moon over. But he didn't photograph well. He looked petulant. Besides, it wasn't his face, it was the expression, the warmth. She couldn't recall it. She was forgetting him, as he was forgetting her. Of course, he must think it was hopeless. What had she done to encourage him?

He lived in Denver. Three months, before he'd be back for the spring performance. He was always in it. Strange how she'd never noticed him until now. Yet he was in all her old programs. Someone looking in her files might think she had been in love with him for years.

It was February. She could fly to Denver, catch a performance, send him a flower, pretend that she happened to be in town. Time was slipping away. It was all supposed to be settled by now. She threw herself into dance classes. Her teacher eyed her, whether pleased or wondering what was up, she couldn't tell. The performance had been a good one. A lot of the students had caught fire. Suddenly she had to be good. Technique was beyond her, but confidence wasn't. Tell a story, she thought to the mirrors. What does your body say?

He wasn't in the Denver phone book. For a horrible day she thought she had the city wrong and she didn't dare ask which was the right one. Then there was no way to contact him. The world had come between them. Finally she thought to look him up in the dance directory. There was his address, the same as an architect's with the same last name in the Denver City phone book. His father? Living at home at his age? And with his wife? He was over thirty. A real man should have his own address. Was it possible he got bothered a lot and just had his dad's address to discourage women? How embarrassing. Just one of the crowd, girlie.

Well, he could have called too. He hadn't, that should tell her something. But maybe he was just shy. He was a married man, she had every right to sneer at him if he made a move.

Serena smiled conspiratorially before class and said "Don't let me forget. Someone wants to meet you. From the cast party. He gave me his number."

Tina felt wild hope.

"Matt Hardage. Do you remember him? He was the tall, bearded guy."

"Is he rich and good-looking?" she asked grumpily.

"Good-looking anyway. Ben liked you too."

"Who was Ben? How did I miss all these men?" It figured. Eighty guys must have fallen in love with her, just when she was concentrating on somebody else. A month ago she would have been happy. Right now it was merely irritating. Might as well not cut herself off from the rest of the world. She knew plenty of fools who did that for a married man. Now she knew how it happened. Well, she'd keep her options open. Go out on a few dates.

She wanted to do something. Fly to Denver and see Paul dance. Send him a rose, with a verse. She had read one somewhere, Shakespeare.

And this I ne'er shall know, but live in doubt
Till my bad angel fire my good one out

The sonnet sounded right. She tracked it down in a book of complete works. She would never know how he felt until her bad, feminine side overcame her pride. She looked up the criticisms to see if it applied. Fire out was a synonym for venereal disease. Well, how charming. And apparently the sonnets had been written to a young man. Surprise, Shakespeare was a flit. Paul would have suspected Reg of sending the rose. They shared a dressing room. Wouldn't that be great? Damn, anyway.

She should have tossed him a real rose in the ballet. One with inch long thorns. And said, "Yes Paul, it's real."

And let him follow through. If he didn't, fine. Forget it. She was a fool. She wouldn't pursue him.

But she'd never had the chance. Damn Paul's wife. If she'd stayed at home with the kid, instead of coming to the party, Tina would have had a chance.

* * * *

Performance night.

Of course she was the first one on stage. Only for a minute alone. If she could just get through it the rest would be easy. Thank God the lighting was dim. Reg gave her a wink, sweet man. What a shame he was gay. He'd be dead in five years, no doubt. AIDS, scourge of the dance world.

Rehearsal had been a joke. The props weren't there, the lights dimmed unexpectedly. Joan, the artistic director, was in a rage. "I'll give the lighting cues myself," she snarled.

Tina went home, ate a cheese sandwich, put on her pancake. At six she was back at the theater, dressing. Two flowers came for her. One from a friend at work, one with no name. Probably from the artistic director. But she could dream.

Why were the first steps so hard? It was obvious what had to happen. She would help him with the divorce, be kind to his daughter, make it easy. There was no reason to hesitate.

Ten minutes before curtain she sneaked a peek at the audience. She always had to, to convince herself they were only people, not mad beasts who would tear her apart if she forgot her steps. She posed for some pictures backstage. Paul was rehearsing, but graciously allowed himself to be photographed. Places were called. She got behind the side drop with her guardsmen.

"I'm going to puke," she whispered.

"Merde," came the whispered reply. Why should they worry? They'd never been on stage before.

The curtain opened, the lights went up, and suddenly she forgot the audience. Absurdly, she thought only of Paul and his deep eyes. Why not? He had ensorcelled the audience as well. She exited on cue. It was over.

He gave her a smile and a squeeze backstage. "That was easy, wasn't it?"

*   *   *   *

The drop came down late on the Ballroom scene and almost knocked her to the floor. It was pitch black. "Shit!" she snarled. Dragging herself up just in time to smile as the curtain opened.

She forced herself to generate energy as she took her place in the dance. Paul came and took his place beside her. She batted her eyelashes fetchingly, catching him by surprise. His mouth twitched, but he managed not to laugh. Juliet danced fatefully his way. He turned to look.

Reg wasn't there where he should be, prepared to take Romeo's place. No, he was on the other side of the stage, watching the action. Paul gave her a helpless look. She nodded quickly, hoping Reg would come to his senses before they had to dance again. The music started, she paraded confidently across the floor and Reg finally caught up with her. "Sorry," he mumbled. "I'll get you for this," she whispered. Some idiot stepped on her train. She stood stock still until he got off. The rest passed without mistakes.

She watched the end from backstage. Some of the peasants missed their cue. One of the lines was manned only by two desperate-looking girls. The missing peasants brushed by her, cursing softly. Probably had been snorting coke in the dressing room.

Paul exited, panting heavily into the wings. She allowed herself to fantasize.

The third act began, rolling to its inevitable conclusion. They got a standing ovation. It had been great. For the first time she understood the concept of teamwork.

The artistic director clapped her hands for attention. "There will be a champagne reception backstage in five minutes. You will attend. You will stay in costume. You will be charming. That is all."

Her costume was stifling. How had the medieval Italians managed it? She rushed out for a drink of water. Paul had beat her to the fountain. "Let me buy you a drink," he teased.

"What a guy." He had pinned his flower to his shirt. "Is that so we can find your heart?"

She went back onstage. Friar Lawrence was struggling with a cork. She helped pour champagne. There was no bartender in sight.

"Tina," Paul touched her arm. "Quick, pass one back." She gave him a full bottle and some glasses. So, he did know her name.

*   *   *   *

The cast party was after the second performance, at the director's lovely custom-built house in a distant suburb. Tina arrived a little late and was annoyed to see that Paul wasn't there. What a waste of time. Well, it wasn't really, she did need to see herself on the videotape. But the magic was certainly gone. All the little kids were clustered on the floor. She sat on the credenza. With her miniskirt she couldn't really settle there, though. She went downstairs after watching her part to get some food.

When she got back Paul was sitting on the credenza. One of the fencers was sitting next to him. This was it. She butted boldly in between. "I was here first." Paul smiled at her. He was wearing casual clothes and a pair of wire rim glasses. She was amused and touched by the sight of them. He must be near-sighted. He did have a squint. He looked like an accountant. An accountant who lifted weights.

They made awkward conversation. "How long have you been dancing?" he asked. "I never saw you before."

"Years," she said nervously. "But I hate to perform." As a matter of fact the year before she had danced the Nutcracker. He had been in the production. Hadn't noticed a six foot tall redhead? Probably had his mind on other matters.

She noticed a woman across the room glaring at him. At first she thought it was one of the dancer's mothers. She was overweight, forty-ish, with hard features and little eyes. Her clothes did not conceal these flaws. Some women should simply not wear pants. And no woman should wear purple polyester stretch pants. Suddenly she saw the little girl beside her and realized. Paul's wife. My god. Never seen her this close up before. She really was old. And homely. And clearly hostile and intimidated by the young dancers around her. Where on earth had they met? Maybe Paul had needed surgery and she had caught him at a low point in his life. And cemented the relationship with the daughter he adored.

Tina leaned casually against Paul. She might have been leaning against a wall. No response. Well, hell. She imagined them kissing in the guest bedroom. Imagined his wife catching them, slapping Tina viciously. No one would be on her side, of course. She was chasing a married man. If there was a fight she would be the one thrown out, even though she had danced there for years. Everyone would snicker at her afterwards.

The director's Irish wolfhound bounded in among the screaming children. Paul's daughter tried to pet it. Paul's wife, looking slightly frantic, tried to push it away.

Tina jumped up and grabbed the dog's collar. "Don't worry, he's a friendly dog."

The woman glared at her. "If that red-haired dog doesn't get away from my child somebody's going to get decked." They exchanged a look of perfect understanding.

Tina stayed a while and smiled and talked to Serena and the older dancers. He was leaving tonight. Going back. And that was it until Spring Performance.

She left early, so as not to be too pathetic and obvious. After fifteen minutes she drove back, pretending she had forgotten her scarf. He was gone and they had rewound the tape. She watched her entrance again. Someone came and sat beside her. Paul. She smiled, suddenly feeling much better.

Then his wife came hurrying up the stairs after him. So much for that. The party was winding down. It was a long drive back. She would be really depressed if she had to watch him leave. Depressed and obvious. She gathered up her purse and said goodbye to the director.

Joan swatted her on the rear. "Behave now." Did she know? Did everybody?

Tina passed the wife on the way out. She was clutching her child and remarking to another wife, "You can't watch them every minute. But they don't usually mean to get into trouble."

Then it was a long, cold drive back to the city, wondering all the way how she'd managed to miss her cue. How had it turned out that here she was alone, while the obvious impediment hadn't even moved an inch?

Dinner Date

She wants him, he can tell. Her eyes sparkle, her lips are red and full. She leans closer, giving him a clear view down the front of her blouse. She's burning. But she doesn't know it yet.

Twenty-three, far younger than his wife, a firm, bouncy body not worn out by child-bearing. Amazingly blonde and tall. Taller than him.

He is different from any man she has ever known. So romantic. So intent. An Indian. They are at an Indian restaurant. He orders for her. She wouldn't know what to get. She surrenders to his wisdom blissfully. How different from the other men she has dated. Boys, really. So full of themselves. So loud and talkative. So whiny and complaining, as if to their mother.

He does not speak of himself. Deftly he turns away questions and instead draws her out. Such a pretty girl. As face like a flower, doesn't she have a man? How can she not be married?

Twenty-three and certainly no virgin. Even so, such a creature, so lovely and blonde, with such perfect teeth, she could be married. She makes a great deal of money, over $30,000 a year. Riches. For that, some poor man would overlook the rest.

She must be a whore by nature. Boyfriends. Many of them, although she does not say so. They mean nothing to her. She admits it candidly, taking his breath away. They are boys, not sophisticated,. Very well then what more could he want?

His cousin had told him of such women. Goddesslike, beautiful, insatiable. He had not believed it.

How gentle he is, how quiet. How ridiculous he makes all that macho posturing. She closes her eyes, imagines minarets, the perfume of night flowers, whispered poetry, wine. He has small hands for a man. Caressing her face…Dark eyes, dark long lashes like a woman's.

He has endured many hardships, they have left their mark in sorrow. A dead wife? She does not imagine a living wife. A life in the slums. The slow hard path of self-education, and now a businessman. One of the company's suppliers.

The witch. She is teasing him. She sucks up her drink, some vile concoction of fruit juices, and tells him how nervous she is with her roommate gone. All alone, she says. It frightens her.

He takes her hands, sqeezes it. I won't let you be afraid, he says. She smiles, but appears not to see the point.

Why this ridiculous custom of sitting across from each other? Next to her he could allow his hands free license. He presses her knee with his under the table. She moves her leg. These tables are so small, she laughs.

Goat has a horrible strong flavor. How can something that eats grass taste so bad? And she's starving too. Better have dessert. She eats the vegetable glumly. She doesn't really like vegetables, but it's all she's going to get. Why didn't she order chicken? It's hard to screw up chicken.

Excitement has made her lose her appetite. She is ready. He knows it. Women too, have powerful urges. Another drink. She knows she is supposed to be a lady, but she will forget.

The room is a lovely soft-lit haze. She probably shouldn't have had that drink. Everything glows. She will be sorry tomorrow. She flips her hair back, that cute little way she has. His eyes follow her. He is saying something about a wife. Whose wife?

He marveled at the ease of it all. His father's son, he had always had it easy. A wealthy businessman's son. Life was good. And seeing this glorious creature, late at night, in the office. For a moment he had lost himself.

But she had agreed. Let that remind him, she was only a woman after all. He allowed his mind to stray into the acts he would cajole out of her. Only a little more wine. She might instruct him, for all he knew. Not really a whore, she was more like a child with a fabulous new toy.

Who said all foreign men were all macho assholes? Hispanic men certainly were. European men, though often charming, were also. But here was a whole new culture. A gentler, more natural way of living. More accepting, more forgiving.

She looked at him in this new light. No, not tonight. That was one of her little rules. Not this time, not the first time. He might think less of her.

It was now. The time, the place. He would go to her apartment. His wife knew better than to question him. Still, it would be kind to warn her he would be later than usual tonight.

A little lie, she would know it was a lie. It was a kind of respect, not to flaunt this in her face. She was his wife, after all.

In the taxi then, he would take what was his. Women understood force. She stood up. Almost six feet tall. For a moment he felt doubt. But only for a moment.

VACATION

The signs had been there from the beginning, as even Christine had to admit. Melody was just impossibly self-centered. True, the vacation in Europe had been her idea. But Jeanette and Christine were doing her a favor by coming along. If they hadn't, Melody couldn't have gone. She would have had no one to go with.

Christine was a very sensitive person. She felt things deeply and in a more complicated way than most people. She had formless misgivings about the whole venture, while Melody seemed to have none at all, not about the vacation or anything else. On reflection, Christine decided it would be best to also invite Jeanette.

"Jeanette is a very nice person and I think she'd be really fun to have along," she explained to Melody. "You know, I'm a very cautious person and I really hope this trip will teach me to take risks. I've allowed myself to get shut off. Maybe now I'll be more open to what the world has to offer."

It was always best to be clear about one's goals.

"It's not that she means to be thoughtless," Christine told Jeanette. Christine never spoke evil of anyone, not even of Ted Bundy. There was always some good quality to accentuate and they never meant some of the really awful things they did. "Of course, she's been there before and knows all the interesting things to see. I just feel, you know, that she might overwhelm me."

"Well," said Jeanette firmly, "We won't allow that to happen. You are simply too nice for your own good. You mustn't let people walk all over you. I think we agreed that's one of your issues to work on. And I'm certainly not sticking to some stupid itinerary."

"Well, she did ask us what we wanted to do."

"And handed us this list. It's obvious she wants to take control of the whole vacation. Well, little Miss Melody is in for a surprise. I think it was a good thing you invited me."

They planned their trip over a long dinner, starting out with a bottle of wine at Jeanette's coldly modernistic condo. "Well, I shall never find true love again," said Christine for the fiftieth time. "I expect to get married someday, probably to a much older, wealthy man. But there will be no love in the marriage."

"Sounds like prostitution to me." said Melody with no apparent respect for Christine's feelings. "Why don't you just get a good job and marry a much younger horny man? At least you'd have some fun."

"I don't think I was meant to be happy that way," replied Christine with a pensive sigh.

"Well, that's rough." Melody tipped back her glass. "I don't think I was meant to be hungry."

"Yes, I think it's time to eat," said Jeanette with a significant look at Christine. "Where shall we go?"

"Oh you decide, you decide. I really don't care."

"Okay, Chinese," volunteered Melody.

"Oh no, not Chinese. I had Chinese last week. I simply couldn't eat Chinese twice." Christine was repelled by the idea.

Jeanette said nothing, allowing the situation to unfold, a knowing smile on her face.

"Well, where do you want to go, then?" asked Melody.

"You decide."

"Mexican."

"Oh, no. That's impossible. We're having a Mexican lunch at the office next week."

"The new French restaurant?"

"Oh, I think we should save our money."

"We're back to Chinese, then."

"Well, if you want to so much. But I couldn't eat a bite."

At the restaurant they had the buffet dinner. Christine took a large plate and forced herself to eat it all. Melody, of course, wolfed down her food and refused to acknowledge how miserable she was making everybody.

*   *   *   *

They arrived in Paris after a long, tiring flight. There was a certain pace to civilized life that Melody did not seem to appreciate. One simply didn't rush. Life was to be savored, like the finest brandy. Melody did not savor. She gobbled. She threw herself into things without forethought, bleached curly hair flying in every direction, totally unconcerned with possible consequences. She even enjoyed the airline food.

"Melody please, the plane ride was very exhausting. I really feel that I need a nap."

"Oh no, you don't want to take a nap now. It's eleven o'clock in the morning here. If you take a nap now you'll screw up your internal clock for the whole trip. Come on. What are you waiting around for. We're in Paris, cultural center of the universe."

"Oh all right," Christine sighed wearily. "I'm sure you know what you're doing. After all you've been here before."

Jeanette looked significantly at her.

"You shouldn't give in," she whispered loudly.

"Oh, it'll be all right. We're just suffering from jet lag. Why don't we just change and go, like Melody wants?"

"Change into what?" asked Melody. "I'm wearing this." She was dressed in jeans and a shabby old black jacket. "Try not to look wealthy whatever you do. You'll just get your pocket picked."

"Well, I guess you didn't pack a lot of things." said Christine. "Not that that's bad, I mean. I sure I don't need half the things I brought. I just like to make a good impression. I know that's superficial, really, but it gives me confidence. I'll just take a quick shower and be right out."

She came back a moment later. "We don't have a shower in there. And there's a weird little toilet."

"That's the bidet, dear," said Melody, flipping through a guidebook, marking entries with her pencil.

"Well, I don't think this is a very good hotel room. There aren't enough towels and there isn't a shower and the heat doesn't work."

"What'd you expect for fifty bucks?" asked Melody unsympathetically. "The Ritz?"

Christine's eyes filled up with tears. "I just don't see how I can live like this."

"Oh calm down, you're just jet-lagged."

"Well, I think Christine has a valid point." Jeanette said firmly. "Don't worry Christine. We'll see that we get our money's worth." She rooted grimly in one of her three suitcases, pulling out outfit after coordinating ourfit. "There certainly isn't much closet space."

"Use mine, I didn't bring anything that would wrinkle."

"Thank you," said Jeanette coldly. While Melody used the bathroom she said, "She certainly is making a big production out of her charity."

"I'm sure she didn't mean to be rude," said Christine doubtfully.

They went downstairs after Jeanette and Christine had bathed and ate an unsatisfactory lunch in the dining room. Jeanette was surprised when someone's white poodle nosed her under the arm.

"They let them in restaurants here." explained Melody.

"Oh, that's disgusting." said Christine, turning pale.

"I see why people say the French are filthy," snapped Jeanette.

"I just can't eat." Christine pushed her plate away.

"OK, let's go then." Melody was off like a rocket.

"She's so energetic," said Christine, smiling weakly.

"She's a pain in the ass," remarked Jeanette. "I hate to say this, but I think she may be on something. Did you see how much she ate? And how scrawny she is? That's not normal. If she's carrying something we could all be in trouble."

Christine looked at her with horrified eyes. "Oh my God, prisons here are terrible. Do you really think she is?"

"I think we'd better look through her luggage. I know it sounds paranoid, but how well do we really know her?"

*   *   *   *

"Well, the museum is closed. You really have to stay on schedule in Europe, everything has such weird hours."

"I would really like to see the Arc de Triomphe." ventured Christine timidly.

"Yuch, what a dreary bore."

"I think that sounds nice," said Jeanette firmly.

"OK, it's right on the Champs-Elysees, so we could do some people-watching."

"Maybe we could sit down for a while first. I know I'm being a wimp, but I tire so easily."

Later, at a little sidewalk cafe, Christine expressed her disappointment. "Well, I must confess this is not up to my expectations. This is not the Paris of my dreams. It's almost dirty."

"You'd call this dirty? And you've been to New York? What about the subway? Isn't it unbelievably nice compared to New York?"

"Well, I certainly never ride the subway in New York. It's so dangerous. I'm sure Paris is very wonderful. I don't mean to sound ungrateful."

"I'm hungry," announced Jeanette. "And this pace you're setting is extremely tiring."

"Well, I guess I'm just excited. It's so great to be back. Let's see, there's a nice restaurant around here somewhere."

"We are scarcely dressed for a restaurant." Jeanette pointed out.

"Are you kidding? This isn't Tulsa, it's Paris. They don't mind you wearing jeans. It convinces them of their total superiority."

The restaurant was lovely. The waiters wore long aprons, there were painted lamps and a stained glass ceiling.

"I feel so unchic," murmured Christine. She was sure the waiter had sneered at them.

"God, this food has really gone downhill." said Melody.

The man in the booth next to them began to lick his plate.

*　　*　　*　　*

Notre Dame was on the agenda the next day. Melody was up at 7:00 AM.

"Well this is vacation, I'll be getting up when I feel like it," said Jeanette.

"It's awfully early," said Christine gently, but with the faintest hint of annoyance.

"Oh go back to bed. I'm going to Vincennes. I already saw Notre Dame. Twice in fact. It's lovely and all, but I've never been to Vincennes. Shall we meet at the D'Orsey, say at 1:00?"

She was gone before they could answer.

Jeanette and Christine looked at each other.

"My, it's hard to believe she's not tired."

"Well, I certainly don't know what she thinks she's doing." snapped Jeanette. "This is an obvious power play. Do it her way or she'll desert us. Well, we certainly don't need her to guide us through the Metro. I think this will be an ideal time to make sure she's not taking anything." She crossed the room and began digging through Melody's bag.

"Do you think this is right?" asked Christine nervously.

"I certainly don't intend to suffer for someone else's irresponsible behavior."

The search didn't take long, since she'd brought only one small carry-on bag. They found nothing.

"I hate to say this, but I think she's a little neurotic. Look at this, hardly any clothes and we'll be gone for three weeks. And if she isn't taking pills she must be sticking her finger down her throat. We may have to confront her with it."

"We should leave that for a professional, I think." said Christine nervously. The word 'confrontation' had always frightened her.

"Of course, you're right. We'll just suggest it. After all her life is not our responsibility."

*   *   *   *

Melody took them to a little restaurant that night.

"It's real Paris," she told them, "With a band in a dark little cellar. It's near the Pompidou."

The Pompidou was not in a nice section of Paris. They had changed for dinner. Jeanette and Christine looked dressy but casual in wool pants. Melody was in a black minidress with a deep V back and ridiculous earring made of gobs of gold foil stuck with huge fake jewels. She looked absurd, but that was her problem, they had decided after a brief consultation.

There were giant groups of rough-looking students and winos all around the Pompidou. Christine clutched her purse tightly and walked with her eyes fixed in front of her. A boy sidled up to Melody.

"Hello baby," he said hopefully.

"Goodbye baby," she snorted.

"Crazee," he muttered sadly as he walked away.

Well, what did she expect, wearing that dress?

"I think we're lost," snapped Jeanette.

"Well, let me see." She stopped, propped one black-stockinged leg up and examined her map. "Whoops, we're going in just exactly the wrong direction. We'll have to go back."

"Oh no. No, we can't. I am not going back in that area. Those awful people. That awful man, I don't know what he wanted. I think he thought you were a prostitute, Melody."

"In his dreams, maybe." She walked off without a backward glance.

Christine and Jeanette looked at each other.

"Well," said Christine.

"I knew it would come to this," said Jeanette grimly. "Don't worry. I'll handle it."

The restaurant was perfect. A little cellar club with African music. They ordered, then Christine vanished for twenty minutes in the restroom.

"Do you really think that dress is appropriate?"

Melody raised one eyebrow. "More appropriate than pants, I should think. Only lesbians wear them to nightclubs in France."

Jeanette gasped in horror, then realized that of course she must be joking.

"Surely you can see, Melody, that Christine and I are quietly and tastefully dressed. I realize you didn't bring many clothes, but you could always borrow from us. Those earrings, they're really tasteless. They look like something a kid would buy."

Melody smiled faintly at a man eating alone across from them.

"You know, we haven't met a single man since we got here. And I heard women got hit on all the time."

"Melody, hasn't it occured to you that Christine and I are very uncomfortable?"

"Sounds like somebody's got a problem. Glad it isn't me." Their appetizer arrived and she began to eat the shrimp, head, eyes, shell and all, with an expression of great thoughtfulness. The hostility was all too evident to Jeanette.

"Look Melody," snapped Jeanette. "We could all have a problem with you walking around dressed like a slut. I certainly won't protect you if a situation occurs."

Melody looked blank. Struck dumb with astonishment, no doubt. Jeanette almost regretted her words, but little forcefulness was needed to get through to people like Melody. "Frankly Melody, you're selfish bitch. You haven't given one thought to Christine's and my happiness. You just don't seem to care."

"I believe you have grasped the situation completely, Jeanette. You are sitting in a lovely dinner club in the most beautiful city in the world. If you're not happy, I'm not going to lose any sleep over it."

Christine chose this moment to return. "Oh Melody, I think you've just misunderstood Jeanette's honesty. We don't mean to be critical. I mean nobody's perfect, I'm certainly not, I know I have lots of faults. We just think things would be more comfortable if you'd just cooperate."

Melody sighed, and smiled across the room at another man. There was not the slightest indication that she'd absorbed a word they'd said.

*   *   *   *

The next morning they were going on to Rome. Melody read a magazine as they packed their bags.

"You could help." snapped Jeanette.

"Excuse me? Didn't I suggest you take only one bag?"

Jeanette stood up. "I am not going to tolerate any more of this. I thought last night that it was just the wine, but I can see-"

Melody stood and picked up her bag.

"Where are you going?" squeaked Christine.

"To find new traveling companions." said Melody, with only the slightest trace of sarcasm.

"You can't just desert us!"

"Why not?"

"You're behaving like a spoiled child!" said Jeanette.

"Well, then I guess you won't have to put up with my spoiled behavior any more."

"But how are we going to get to Rome?"

"On the train, I imagine."

"We don't know anything about it. You planned evrything."

"I guess you'll have to figure something out."

"Well, I just think everyone's over-reacting." said Christine hastily. "I'm sure it can all be worked out. It would be so expensive to rebook hotel rooms at this late date."

"I'm sure," remarked Melody. She sat back down, opened a magazine and ignored them completely.

On the train, she appeared not to notice their struggles to heave their bags up on the train rack. Some unshaven man helped her with hers and explained their connections in great detail.

She was not reassuring when Christine discovered the train had no seatbelts. "They don't have many fatal crashes. And a seatbelt wouldn't be much help in one anyway."

"Oh don't say that. I don't know how I will sleep at all tonight. This is just impossible. I didn't realize travel was so unsafe here."

"Do you really think you should have encouraged that man?" snapped Jeanette.

"He's just a guy," said Melody.

*   *   *   *

When they arrived she waited patiently while they unpacked.

"Ready to go?"

"Well I really think we need something to eat first."

She shrugged. "See you." She was out the door without a backward glance.

"I wonder where she thinks she's going. You can't just wander around Rome like you own it. I can't believe she wearing that miniskirt. I wouldn't be surprised if she gets attacked. Some women bring it on themselves"

They lunched at a very bad, overpriced cafe. Jeanette argued over the bill and lost. "This is ridiculous. A charge for napkins. Next time I'll bring my own."

"Where should we go?" It was three in the afternoon.

"Well, I don't know, what's in the guidebook?"

"I left it at the hotel."

"Really, Christine. What about the map?"

"Well," sniveled Christine, "I don't see why it's all my responsibility. And it was really selfish of Melody to run off with the only map."

"I knew we should have bought one too. Well, we'll just take a taxi to the Coliseum. They'll know how to get there."

The cab cost about twenty dollars, as near as they could figure it. "We must be pretty far away from the sights. We shouldn't have let Melody book the hotel rooms. I can't imagine why she thought she could walk all the way over here."

"Well, I must admit I'm disappointed. I thought it would be bigger."

"Look, isn't that Melody?"

It was. Across the Coliseum, she was talking animatedly to a handsome, dark-haired man.

"I might have known. Anything in pants will do."

"Oh, don't say that. She's just very trusting. Do you think she's in danger?"

"Some people have to learn the hard way. Come along, there's nothing we can do."

They went to a nearby restaurant, where Christine discovered that her pocketbook had been stolen.

*   *   *   *

Melody didn't come home until 2:00 AM. Jeanette and Christine had just fallen asleep after discussing how pushy and rude the Italians were, and what a slut Melody was.

"Isn't Rome great?" Apparently she hadn't been attacked. "I met the greatest guy. We went to a really neat bar. It was great. I love Rome. I think I've lost five pounds."

"Well," sniffed Christine. "I think we all have. The food isn't at all what I expected. It's really kind of bland. I'm dying for a hamburger."

Melody shrugged. "There's a McDonald's near the Spanish Steps."

"You needn't be so sarcastic. I have a right to express my disappointment."

"If you want a hamburger that's where you get it. What's the big deal? Have you been to any museums? There seems to be this gay bondage theme. I mean really, these Renaissance Italians."

*   *   *   *

The next day was the Vatican. Melody was going to meet her new friend. She was irritating enthusiastic.

"The coffee here is terrible." said Christine peevishly at breakfast. "It's like mud." The strain was showing.

"I hope you'll be careful, Melody, although of course it's none of my business. God knows what diseases he has," said Jeanette.

"Oh, trust a medical student to keep himself germ-free," said Melody cheerfully.

"A medical student?" said Christine with awe.

"Melody, let's be realistic." Jeanette put he cup down sharply. "It's very unikely you ran into a future doctor your first day in Rome."

Melody fixed her with a pair of innocent blue eyes. "Well, of course I did. I met him in Emergency over at the student clinic. I was feeling dizzy from all the sun. That's the best way to meet a doctor, don't you think? While they're still students and unmarried." She paused expectantly. "Well, you did realize there had to be a medical school in Rome."

She didn't wait for another cup of coffee.

Christine and Jeanette stared at each other, speechless.

After a moment Christine said wistfully, "Did you hear that? He's a medical student. They'll probably get married. Why is she so lucky?"

"A medical student? Let's get real, Christine. He's obviously lying. He's probably just some sort of aide. And they can't have anything real, not in two days. She's being taken advantage of."

"Well, she's just a very energetic person. I feel so tired. This vacation isn't turning out at all like I thought it would. I think I'm having cramps. I'm going to lie down."

After thinking about facing the terrors of Rome on her own, Jeannette decided the loyal thing would be to nurse Christine through her illness.

Melody bounded in at about two o'clock.

"Oh, I'm glad you're here. I'm moving out. I paid my part of the hotel bill already. Here's the phone number if you need to get a hold of me."

She was packed in two minutes and gone.

"She's moving in with that man. I don't know what dream world she's living in. That man could rape and murder her. She'll be lucky if she keeps her money and passport. These foreigners are always on the lookout for tramps like her."

Christine took a deep, shaky breath. "I'm afraid she's rather cheap."

It was the worst thing she'd ever said about anybody.

ARIANNA'S SHOES

Arianna. There was little doubt in her mind that she would succeed.

She made sure she always looked the part, knew who was who, and had a good address. It didn't matter if you lived in one room in a basement in Sausalito, California, not even a legal rental, with ceilings less than six feet high. You lived in Sausalito and that was all people had to know. That was good enough.

She knew exactly what she wanted and had no doubts that she was worth it. She pursued her goals aggressively. The timid little mice of the world held back, knowing they weren't good enough. She knew the world was hers for the taking. She had what it took. That indefinable something. IT.

She was small and compact, bleached blonde. Blonde got you noticed, it said something about you. She dieted religiously and worked out at the Sausalito Nautilaus. The classes were mostly women, true, but those women had brothers, cousins, even fathers. She would be in a Corvette, with a doctor by her side. A handsome doctor. Kansas City was nothing, it was nowhere. There were not even ladders to climb. The wind blew endlessly through dusty alleys and went nowhere in the end.

But Kansas City was very far away. This was real real real. These people had real money, did real things, jetted to Paris on the Concorde, lunched with Prince Charles. Had small villas in Cap-Ferrat.

"I've been to Paris," said Monica, one of the aerobics women. Not one with connections. Arianna threw her a pitying look, knowing she traveled in coach, stayed in pensiones with the toilette down the hall. That wasn't traveling. It wasn't real. If it wasn't real, Arianna wasn't going to waste time on it.

*   *   *   *

She looked like one of them, the people who got what they wanted. The hidden people. The ones who lifted their little finger and the thing was done. Those of quiet power.

She went to her hair stylist, her manicurist, the popular restaurants in town. If you want to meet the rich, go where they go. Look like they look. Talk like they talk.

She wouldn't play with little boys. The car, the house, the job, they all had to be right. She went to the right shops, the right restaurants, was seen with the right people.

That counted, being seen. When people thought of the financier, or the budding playwright, they also thought of you, sitting next to him, in the witty printed comic-book skirt.

*   *   *   *

On her Sunday morning walk, wearing a bright pink designer stretch pants, low-cut top and serious walking shoes, Arianna noticed the apartment. A real apartment, not a room with a hot plate like her place. It was one bedroom and cheap, because there was no light or view. $750. She elbowed aside the pale scrawny woman, Monica, with a tight smile and handed over her application first. It was made for her.

It wasn't for that tall, pale, cross thing who looked so puzzled and tired.

Her new place was perfect. She only had to find someone who would buy her some decent furniture. She had a fabulous entertainment center courtesy of her last boyfriend, the washed-up management trainee. He hadn't exactly meant to give it to her after the breakup, but she had ended up with it anyway.

Later, Arianna noticed Monica leaving another apartment, closer to downtown with even a view. She demanded to know the cost from the real estate agent who had rented her the original studio apartment. $1400 a month. Ridiculous. It cost twice what she was paying. To think Pale Scrawny Monica was living there.

Then she saw Monica again at an open house for sale. A three-quarter of a million dollar 2-bedroom apartment in a prestigious building, right downtown. That was her goal. It was just a matter of getting there. What on earth was Monica doing there? She stood uncomfortably at the edge of the room as Arianna talked up the real estate agent. A complete fake. You shouldn't try it if you weren't dressed for the part.

"Aren't you renting now?" Arianna demanded and shoved her card into the woman's hand. "I would really like a shot at your apartment when you move. You're Monica, right?"

The woman flushed and nodded. She looked completely flustered. No confidence.

The woman never called. Of course not. She had never moved out. She was nobody. Just a pretender and not even doing that very well.

✳   ✳   ✳   ✳

"What cool shoes," said a little mouse in the grand Ladies' room at Boulevard.

"Thank you," replied Arianna in a chilly voice. They **were** cool shoes, black men's style shoes with silver buckles.

She was annoyed. Her date wasn't going well. The man, a lawyer, didn't seem to notice how special she was. He was totally wrapped up in himself, talking loudly about lawyer things that didn't matter to anyone. And the restaurant rubbed her the wrong way, even the bathroom. The ceiling twelve feet up. It was bigger than her living room. And better art on the walls.

Suddenly she noticed pale Monica, combing her limp hair at the sink, who had on the same shoes as she did. No one had complimented **her**. No one even noticed the shoes.

Because it wasn't the shoes. Wasn't JUST the shoes. You had to have the shoes, of course. To prove you belonged. You knew what the cool shoes were. But the coolest shoes in the world couldn't save the Monicas.

Because they were what they were. And they weren't going anywhere.

*   *   *   *

"What if everyone were more beautiful than me?" said the woman in the next chair at the salon. Linda? her name was. Or Laurel. Of course she was pretty, if only in an ordinary way. "How depressing. What do those bottom people think of themselves?"

"I don't have that problem," snapped Arianna.

"Lived here 11 years," said the little Vietnamese manicurist. "Haven't met a rich guy yet. Did you know Laurel is from Kansas City, too?"

Arianna glared at Laurel. They had absolutely nothing in common. Wasn't it obvious?

No one makes it without an insider. You had to find one, do what it takes. Doesn't matter who else is hanging on his arm, she could make it Arianna.

She smiled knowingly at the guy in the Jag, little Miss Wish She Had It on his arm. She followed them into the Japanese place, brushed by him on the way to the bathrrom, put on lipstick, smiled at herself. She was wearing Diane von Furstenberg. One of her two nice dresses. She didn't have much, but what she had was quality. And it wouldn't be overlooked.

*   *   *   *

Out on her Sunday walk, in her DKNY exercise clothes, Arianna saw the Monica woman again. She was outside the expensive building, the one with the three-quarter million dollar apartment with a fabulous view. She was on her hands and knees. Praying? No, gardening.

"New job?" Arianna asked unkindly.

Monica blinked at her through thick perscription sunglasses. "I live here," she said shortly. She pushed away a strand of damp no-color hair and squinted. She obviously didn't remember Arianna at all.

Arianna noticed she was still wearing the cool shoes.

I must get rid of those right away, she thought to herself, as she stalked away without wasting further conversation on the woman.

I'm certainly not like her, thank God.

A Quiet
Neighborhood

The last tenant had disappeared without a trace. Actually, the landlord thought she had drowned in the surf a few hundred yards down the road.

"A total druggie, y'know?" He coughed, scratched an armpit, leered at Rachel. He resembled a balding Syrian brothel-keeper. "She was some kind of porno actress. Real dumb. Used to swim alone all the time. Skinny-dipping. Guy up the road says he saw her out there a couple of nights,"

If the guy up the road was still around, Rachel saw no sign of him. It was a very quiet neighborhood. Cars came and went, but she rarely saw people out. There was a connecting bus to the city. It came every two hours or so, in spite of the sign that scheduled it hourly. Once in a while she'd see a man sauntering down to meet it, dressed in dirty work clothes and carrying a lunch box. Sometimes kids would come out to wash their cars, but only in groups and always playing loud music, as if to frighten away evil spirits.

Some of the houses were deserted, she was sure. Night or day, there were no lights. The cars in front never left the curb. The streets were cracked and overgrown, the wild gradually overtaking the city. A few more years and they would excavate this lost suburb of Los Angeles and puzzle over its final days.

She brought her dog Merle for protection and companionship. Merle was old, fat, frowzy and arthritic. She wheezed a lot and stumbled, but she was big and she loved Rachel loyally, perhaps the only creature in the world that truly did.

Rachel had left her boyfriend Doug to his ratty apartment in the city. She left, finally, because he didn't care whether she stayed or went, as long as it was no trouble to him either way. He knew she hadn't left for another man. There wasn't one that wanted her. She was nearly thirty, with a pale, undistinguished face, frizzy hair and a body that was a little too plump. After she left it would be all downhill for her. She'd never get anybody better. He knew it. She knew it. Everybody knew it.

The dead girl's things were still stored in the crawl space. Somehow the landlord had overlooked them. Or maybe he thought she'd be back for them. Salvation Army clothes, out of date, with a strange smell. Rachel knew the smell came from being stored in the damp and dark. That had to be it. But she couldn't help thinking of death germs, exuding through the air, infecting everything they touched with doom. Soon people would avoid her like they would a plague victim. She would die in the street without help. Her body would be robbed and left to rot where it lay.

The duplex came furnished. The first day Rachel had turned over all the cushions looking for bloodstains. She was sure that the girl, Irene, had been murdered right there in the apartment and her body buried in the fields somewhere. Her spirit still haunted the dirty carpets, the cracked walls, the linoleum, the plastic kitchen chairs.

Rachel's cat became unfriendly the first week. It bit her when she tried to pick it up and escaped growling into the fields. Merle looked at her with big worried dog eyes, as if uncertain of her smell.

It was hard to get to sleep at night, in the absolute dark, in a dead woman's bed. The refrigerator would make noises like footsteps, or noises that could disguise footsteps, or stop suddenly with a silence that would wake her. When she fell asleep in the hot afternoons she had terrible dreams.

She hoped to meet new people, but never did. The boys would watch her house sometimes. They must know she lived alone. Like Irene, would she simply vanish? Who would look for her if she did? The police might not even be notified. Merle stayed out at night, guarding the weedy yard.

She called her friend Jackie finally. Jackie was more of an acquaintance than a friend, but she was always eager to see people, if only to hear what bad things had happened to them. Jackie sounded curious on the phone. Not concerned, not friendly, just curious.

At seven o'clock there was a knock on the door. Expecting Jackie, she opened it. It was the man from the bus stop. Too thin. Hair too long. Shirt hanging open. Grinning. One missing tooth in front.

"Is Irene here?" His eyes were very fixed.

"Irene doesn't live here," Rachel said nervously. "I guess she moved."

"I've seen you around, haven't I?" asked the man. He stuck out his hand. "I'm Joe Farnsworth. I've seen you on the beach."

"Rachel Ward," she said, not wanting to. He let go of her hand very slowly. He smelled, kind of. "I've never been down to the beach. You must be thinking of that other girl."

The gap-toothed grin. Couldn't he afford a dentist? Didn't he care? He needed a shave, too.

"Some people go skinny-dipping out there," he said knowingly. "You sure that wasn't you?"

"Yes, I'm sure," she said with a stiff smile.

"Maybe it was your roommate. Or do you have one?"

"Yes," she said quickly. She could tell he knew she was lying.

"I think I left my shovel over here. Mind if I look around for it?" His eyes were rabidly bright.

There are charmed circles. Everything goes right in them. She was living in a cursed circle. Everyone who stepped inside it would go temporarily insane, and once back out, wouldn't understand why. They'd blame it on her somehow.

"It's not here. The landlord took everything for back rent. I'm sorry. Maybe you could talk to him."

"I think I know where I left it." He started to push his way in. Merle waddled in from the kitchen, growling. Jackie drove up at that moment, her headlights illuminating them.

"That's my roommate," she said quickly.

"Bitch," he said, retreating down the drive. "Thieving slut!" he yelled. He stood a while down the road, watching Jackie get out of the car.

I won't let it get to me, she told herself. Transient type. They always picked on her. Thought she should be grateful for their attentions. They could see she didn't get much.

"Who was that?" asked Jackie.

"Some weirdo." She closed the screen door. "He wanted the woman who used to live here. I wish he'd go away."

"Well, then don't encourage him," said Jackie practically. "Got any beer?"

Jackie was short, chubby and bouncy. She was not really blonde. She slept with anything male that breathed. Probably she slept with Doug. Sex was a competitive sport with her. She was loud and talkative and thought she had many friends.

"God, I hope that's not the best you can do in this crummy neighborhood. Jesus, this place is depressing. Is this really better than living with Doug?"

Rachel shrugged.

"Look at that couch. Did you pull it out of the gutter? At least Doug has nice things. You don't really want this, do you?"

"The last girl that lived here disappeared. They think she killed herself."

"Well, no wonder. What a dump." Jackie swallowed her beer. "You know, I talked to Doug last night," she said tantalizingly.

And probably got him in the sack too, thought Rachel sourly. Jackie had an enormous chest. And she never wore a bra.

"He seemed so sad. He's changed, he really has."

"Jackie, he was trying to get me into bed with another woman."

"Oh, you don't expect me to take that seriously, do you? He was just joking." She put on her pout. "You hurt him. You really did. The poor guy is just crushed. He cried."

Probably on Jackie's giant bosom. Rachel set her beer down and turned the TV on to a horror movie. She shook her head. "It's over. I just have no more feelings for the guy. Well, anyway, that man you saw leaving—Joe—I'm seeing him now. I didn't want to say anything to hurt Doug, but you know how it is."

"How long have you been seeing him?" asked Jackie eagerly.

"For a couple of months," lied Rachel boldly. "He's getting a divorce."

She closed the door behind Jackie at one o'clock and listened to her car roar away. She checked the locks and let Merle inside. Joe wouldn't be back. That was logical. She felt strange now about telling that story about him being her boyfriend. As if he might have been listening. Might come back, expecting her to follow through.

She got out a steak knife and lay it near her on the end table. If only she had a gun. She didn't want to turn off the comforting sound of the TV. But only the horror movie was still on. The murdered woman's body lay alone in her penthouse apartment, discovered only by flies.

She could go to bed in the waiting dark, listening for the sound of footsteps sliding on the carpet, faint thuds from the kitchen. Here she could at least run out the front door if she heard him break in.

Merle settled heavily on the carpet beside her, breathing loudly.

Where could she run to, if she had to? The weeds in the yard tripping her. The blank impassable doors of nearby houses, twinkling stars the only witnesses to a knife that rose and fell methodically.

In the adjacent fields, where the weeds are overgrown, slink stray mangy dogs. Rustling the bushes by the footpath. Panting. The long grasses rustle, but there is no wind. The sky is cloudy, the air humid and still. The light comes from everywhere but the sky.

Did anyone really live in the houses? Or did they all disappear long ago like the dinosaurs? Leaving only the vacuumed white carpets and the two car garages?

At midnight the lamp shakes and wavers. There is a rumbling from the floor. Is it an earthquake? A truck on the overpass? Her neighbor being strangled, fighting for her life?

On the flickering screen the body was decaying, swollen and horrible. Rachel turned the sound down to a faint mumble. But that wouldn't deter anyone. She turned it up again.

Flies buzzed. Her lamp cast a sullen, orange glow. She kept it on all night. Her bulbs burned out frequently with an abrupt PING! and she would wake up, wondering if someone had found the breaker box.

She drowsed, Merle beside her.

* * * *

From the walls they came. The thin people, the narrow people. The People between the Walls. Slender as pipe cleaners, but invisible. They came to wrap their long twisted fingers around her neck and invisibly choke her breath away in the hot, oxygenless summer air.

Gliding over the carpet with their bent feet, they leaned down and whispered to her. Soon you will be with us.

Someone's scratching. Scratching on the wall. Trapped inside the walls of the house she had died in. The last tenant. Still here.

Small, with pale blue eyeshadow, bad skin and frizzy blonde hair. She smiled uncertainly from the edge of the room.

We never really die. All the religions say so. Something remains forever. And how reasonable that certain people are sacrificed, rather than others. Those with no family. No relatives. A lonely woman, a woman without a man. Prowling the bars. Always searching. Always hopeful.

With that desperate look that asks for trouble. That lures the wrong kind.

My prayers have been answered. Prayers born in the trash bins and gutters. In alleys and dust. Crumbled with scraps of paper in the streets and cigarette butts.

Irene wants to live again. Because no one want to die. Not even a sleazy porno actress, half awake to the tune of the radio. Vodka in her morning orange juice.

Static woke Rachel up.

*   *   *   *

The radio in her Nova worked just as well as the car. Yellow, rattling and rusting, it barely got Rachel down the freeway three times a week, horns blasting as cars swerved around her.

"—four of the gunman's victims. Samuel Brady, area businessman and father of two, was the first to be discovered—"

Why was it always peaceful, reliable fathers of young children who got gunned down? Why didn't real SOB's ever get massacred? Like her boss Herbie. He was an ugly little tyrant, overweight and blind in one eye. Each word he uttered suggested that whenever she used the bathroom she was really snorting coke, or screwing the delivery boy in the basement. Surely such a personality would eventually goad a disturbed person to violent deeds. Was it just that he knew better? Knew who not to push? Or maybe he would be automatically recreated, area businessman and father of two, brutally slain by a psychotic female clerk.

"—apparently she was always a loner, living in a fantasy world with a man she called Joe. Police expressed disbelief at the condition of the apartment she lived in—"

Who, in this climate, would buy a bright orange carpet? A film of dog hairs covered it. She dreamed of acres of white carpet, carefully vacuumed, abstract paintings picking up the color scheme, a swimming pool.

She pulled into the parking lot by the bookstore. They shared a front with a pawnshop, dust grimy on the set of drums in the window.

Wanda was already there, staring at her through thick glasses with pebble green eyes.

"Herbie's looking for you," she said, with no particular inflection. Live or die, rain or shine, it was all the same to Wanda. She had a husband. A house. One kid. Something to fill up her life.

"Rachel!" A hoglike bellow. Herbie was in the back room. "Where have you been? Getting your beauty sleep? Busy with your boyfriend? These books need shelving. They should have been done last week." There were sweatstains under the arms of his shirt. Yellow sweatstains. He reminded Rachel of a clerk at the YMCA. She stared at him dumbly as he ranted. At his ugly pockmarked face. At the veins in his nose. His voice seemed to come from far away. Then it stopped.

She opened her eyes. She was on the floor. Herbie and Wanda's stupefied faces loomed above her.

"Are you pregnant?" demanded Herbie.

She sat up slowly. "It's my stress medication. I was in such a hurry I forgot to take it."

Herbie was in the back the rest of the morning, slamming books and mumbling to himself about psychos who go on disability and still expect to be paid for the work they didn't do.

*   *   *   *

She ate lunch alone at the Pancake House. She'd spent money she shouldn't have, but she couldn't stay in the shop. Sometimes she walked through the air-conditioned stores, looking and clothes she couldn't afford and being watched suspiciously by sales ladies. Today she was tired and wanted to sit. The slick floors would trip her and she'd leave smears of make-up on crisp white blouses.

The sky was lowering when she came out. It was humid. A man brushed by her, smiling knowingly. He mumbled something she couldn't hear. She walked quickly back to the bookstore. The man followed, maybe a block away. She ran in the door.

Herbie laughed. "Got yourself a new boyfriend? You sure aren't picky."

She was glad to drive down the faceless freeway. Her tank was almost on empty again, or she would have driven on forever. There was a sick feeling in her stomach when she turned off at her exit.

The green trees glittered poisonously after the rain. On the left the fields stretched away. The houses in the development looked empty and still. She pulled up in the cracked driveway. The lawn needed mowing. Someone's scruffy yellow cat was slinking around the garbage cans. A fat woman in a pullover was trying to catch it.

"Here Kitty. Here baby." She smiled at Rachel. "Tiger got out somehow."

"Oh," said Rachel.

"I hope you don't mind."

"No, not at all." Rachel didn't know what to say. Was she supposed to invite this behemoth in? She didn't have anything to offer, not even iced tea. And she was sure to want something stronger to drink.

The fat woman was looking at her. "Did you know that girl? The one that used to live here?"

Rachel shook her head.

"I heard she was killed by one of those Satanist cults. She was real quiet. Kind of like you. Quiet types, you just never know. She was into drugs heavy. You have a boyfriend, honey?"

"Kind of."

"He doesn't live here, does he? I don't ever see him come by. He should treat you more nice. I live right down the street there. My name's Carla. I have a little girl, she's just two. Do you babysit?"

Rachel shook her head, imagining the horror of this woman's house, the smells of her kitchen, her leering husband, the unexplained bruises on her child's body. "I can't any more. It was one of the conditions. You know, of probation."

"Oh honey, that's real rough. I bet you didn't do anything that bad. Joe was on probation a while. We moved out here to get away from all that. We're from Minnesota. I thought California would be just like a dream. But I don't have a car. It's weird, being stuck out here. I barely see another person all day. I thought there'd be more people, somehow." The fat woman smiled at Rachel. She seemed slightly frantic.

"I've got to go, really," said Rachel. "I've got to walk the dog."

*   *   *   *

Spirit catchers live out there in deepest space, near the moon. Collecting all the wishes of all the dead people who weren't really ready to die at all. The frightened little liars, who held in their hate, day after day…Their wishes flew through the empty air. Whispered in unlistening ears. One day fourteen people were killed execution-style in a pancake house and no-one can understand—he was always so quiet—.

It was because he was listening. Listening to the void.

*   *   *   *

The house was dim. Ferns were dying. In the kitchen Rachel smashed roaches with a shoe, tracked down spiders. All the evil little creatures that house evil little thoughts and keep them alive. Still bearing traces of the dead girl, Irene.

There are a lot of roaches in the world.

The milk was out on the counter, spoiled. She didn't remember leaving it there. In fact, she was sure she hadn't. Had the landlord been in, poking around? Or some previous tenant, someone with a key?

She could feel herself becoming small and insignificant, as they pressed in on her with their evil thoughts. Shrinking down to the size of a waterbug. Running hysterically around giant cabinets, slipping through the cracks in the wall, becoming trapped there and dying in a sulfurous cloud of insecticide.

She had to get out of the apartment. Meet some people, have a social life.

Escape the cursed circle she found herself in.

*   *   *   *

It was early yet, and the bar wasn't crowded. Seven o'clock. Only the desperate were on the prowl. And a few weathered, scrawny men, serious drinkers. They smiled lamely at her, if they looked at all.

She sat at the bar with a sour Margarita. She was glad it tasted foul—she'd drink it slower that way. She had enough for two drinks and that was all. Unless she spent her gas money and hoped she had enough to get to work on until payday.

The place looked like a converted homestyle restaurant. Booths, yellow stone walls, hanging glass lamps like something you'd put in the front yard. A wrought iron fence separated the dance floor from the tables. Her face in the mirror looked muddy and undistinguished. It was the tan, gotten on a lawn chair in her weedy, dog-shit covered back yard. She needed a haircut. Or a blow dryer. Or something else that cost money. New shoes, a cell phone, an education, a drink. All of it cost. She could never be an alcoholic. That cost too.

Someone sat next to her. A quiet-looking girl wearing jeans and a tank top, hair pulled back in a barrette. She looked like one of those thin, nervous, overly religious women who forgive their husbands everything. All she lacked was the cross around her neck. She smiled nervously at Rachel. Probably had sat next to her on purpose. The only safe person in the room.

"Kinda quiet."

"Yeah," said Rachel. "Does it get busier?"

"Later on." The girl glanced around the room. "People will come around nine. It'll get livelier. So will I." She tapped her glass. "It helps, man."

"What kind of crowd usually comes here?"

"Real nice. Quiet, sort of." The girl ordered another drink. "I'm Linda."

Rachel introduced herself.

"It's a lot different from the city. The people are mellower. Not so intense. You know."

"You've lived in the city? I've thought of moving further in, but it's so expensive."

"Don't, man. I didn't like it." She gestured vaguely. "The people there are so plastic. So rehearsed. They think bikers are scum."

Rachel supposed she was stuck until some man showed up. Maybe Linda was waiting for a friend.

"Arrogant, that's what they are. People won't accept you for what you are. It's like, well, what can you do for me?"

She had a tattoo, Rachel suddenly noticed. A little pink rosebud over her left breast. The tank top didn't quite cover it.

"I met my old man there, so I can't say it's all bad." She turned and in the light Rachel saw that the mark on her cheek was another tattoo—a heart. "We've been together five years. Hey, I think that's pretty good. Some marriages don't last that long."

Rachel nodded resignedly and sucked down the last of her drink. It was like she wore a sign. Weirdos, bother me. Whether it was the alcohol or whether Linda had been shutting it all in, Rachel couldn't tell.

"We went through some hard times together. Real rough times. Our baby died when it was three months old."

"How awful for you," muttered Rachel. Why call it an it? Didn't Linda remember what sex it was?

"We stayed together through that. I guess we'll last." Her eyes, which had looked blank with innocence, now looked blank with burnt-out brain cells.

"We were both hooked, you know. Addicts, man. I guess it was real hard on our kids. That's what the social worker said anyway. They're OK now, though. We've been through a lot."

"It sounds like it." Probably including criminal charges. "Excuse me, I have to, uh, go." She nodded towards the ladies room.

"Me too!"

Linda followed her right into the paper-festooned stall.

"You're not shy or anything?" she asked.

"Uh, no." She wasn't, really, but the woman gave her the creeps. She was over-eager.

Two girls came in, one loudly proclaiming how proud she was that her kid's father was a Mexican. It was just as good as being white. It was better than being white. Rachel felt nervous. It sounded like the prelude to a fight.

Linda pulled down her jeans, still talking. "I almost died, you know. Came real close. It was a miracle, they said. Here, you flush. "I guess God intended me to live for something."

A warning to others, perhaps. She had known God would turn up in there somehow. She took her turn.

"It's like cosmic balance. My baby died, so I got to live. Or vice versa." She stared intensely at Rachel.

"That's crazy," said Rachel. Linda was grinning in a truly insane fashion. Rachel wondered if she carried a knife. "You're stronger, that's all," she said hastily. "Little babies are vulnerable to a lot of things. They die all the time and no-one knows why, not even the doctors." But who knew. Maybe she'd dropped the damn baby headfirst on the floor, let it starve, let the dogs eat it. "You shouldn't feel guilty."

Linda looked hungrily at her. She didn't look as if she felt guilty at all.

They returned to the bar.

"Another?" asked the bartender pointedly.

"Listen, I got to go," said Rachel. "I don't think my date's showing up."

"I thought you said you were alone."

Rachel pressed her lips together. She didn't remember saying that. Was it so obvious?

"Well it's kind of embarrassing. I mean, he does this all the time."
She forced herself to look mournful. "I know he doesn't mean to hurt
me."

Linda smiled knowingly. "Well fuck him, man. You can have a
good time without him." A short wiry man with greasy black hair had
appeared at her elbow. He was smiling at Rachel.

"This is Mike, my old man. He does Art Photography."

"You have a great face," he said. "What a great tan. Have you ever
modeled?"

She shook her head.

"Why don't you let me take a few test shots? We could go down to
the studio. I have some props set up."

They probably included a bed and a dildo.

"I'd really like to, but I have to check on Bill. He has episodes. You
know," she added, inspired, "Since the war."

In the parking lot she sighed with relief. The ground was shifting
treacherously. Just two drinks and look how she was. Used all her own
money too.

At least she got out alive.

*   *   *   *

Day after day, it was the same. She came home in the last hot light
of the evening, past run-down silent duplexes. Old men lived there,
and died there, and their dogs devoured them. Swollen, spotty bodies
discovered days later, when they had begun to smell.

The black and white TV buzzed and glittered and its metallic voice
announced the luck of gameshow contestants. Did these blonde people
actually inhabit the world of the living, or were they just artificial cre-
ations, plausible enough, but totally alien to the true experience of
humanity?

Reality had slipped a fraction of a notch. The seamlines aren't quite
right, the finish is patchy.

The first step is isolation.

At the end of the bus line, in a row of cheap little duplexes where the chosen are lured, one by one.

*   *   *   *

The next day her car was dead. Hopelessly she looked under the hood. Her battery might be missing. She wouldn't know. Joe got on the bus right after her.

"Hey, neighbor, haven't seen you in a while." He grinned his gap-toothed grin. "Hope you didn't think I was rude the other night."

"Forget it," she said.

Taking this as an invitation, he sat beside her.

"Kind of lonesome out here, isn't it?" They were almost the only people on the bus. "Women shouldn't be alone. But most women know that. They know what's best for them."

"Merle keeps me company." She didn't mention that Merle was a dog.

"I gotta apologize. I got real mad the other night. My girlfriend, Irene, the one that used to live there, she was stepping out on me. Met some rich guy who'd pay the rent. Why are women like that?"

Rachel shrugged. We're all sluts, buddy.

"I showed her, treating me like that."

"Right." Rachel stared out the window.

"Going with any man who had the money. Wanted a nice little house and a car. Bet you'd do it too, if you had the chance."

Was he actually going to offer her one? "Not me, my boyfriend would kill me."

*   *   *   *

She got back late that evening. It was nearly dark. She took Merle for a walk on the beach. Stones and shells littered the sands. And beer cans. People came here often. There were timbers set in rows into the waters, marching lonesomely out to sea. In the smoky grey dusk they wavered and shivered.

The souls of the drowned are trapped in those timbers. Maybe Irene was out here, washed up with the tide. Trapped as close to the shore as she could get, silent and alone, until someone came walking along and listened to the waves.

*   *   *   *

Merle plodded along beside Rachel, keeping her safe. Spindly legs, but big as a house. She splashed clumsily in the surf and nosed at something, whining doubtfully. Smelling someone who wasn't really there. She trotted back heavily to Rachel and they walked back up the street in a darkness so black that she didn't see the man until Merle growled.

"Heel, Merle," she said sharply.

"Heel, Merle," said the man insinuatingly. It might have been Joe. She couldn't tell, in the dark.

*   *   *   *

That night Merle whined until she let her in. The night was still black. The electric company did nothing about the streetlights.

Too nervous to sleep in bed, Rachel lay on the couch. Merle crawled right up beside her, at least seventy-five hairy pounds. She sniffed Rachel's face worriedly and licked her hand, watching her with sad eyes.

Rachel patted her and arranged herself. All around her she pictured housewives in curlers, ghostly in the light of the TV, drinking gin and reading depressing confession magazines. None of them had heard the screams of the murder committed in this very house, as they watched pretend murders on their dim black and white TVs.

*   *   *   *

Spirits blew in the wind, spirits of the dead, their work unfinished. Anger and rage swallowed all their lives, strange desires, hidden fears. Spirit proposals, whispered in living ears, spectral fingers, tugging at living arms. The kingdom of life was ruled by the bullies. The cowards ruled the kingdom of death.

Death was sniffing her face. Death with a stiff white hairy mask, trying to suck the breath from her, or only sniffing her nose like a friendly cat.

She woke to the light of day and the clashing light of the desk lamp. Dismally she switched it off and drew the curtains, not feeling like breakfast.

Merle had managed to crawl nearly to the back door, blood scummed out of her mouth, along with foam.

*   *   *   *

The dog had been poisoned. Miserably she dragged the body to the back yard. Joe had to have done it. And what was Rachel going to do about it? Merle was only a dog. She was old. Who could she call? Who would come? She could imagine the knowing looks on the faces of the police officers.

And how long did you say this man been following you?

*   *   *   *

She didn't go to work that day. When she went to the bus stop the bus never came. A car drove by and said the bus didn't come out there any more.

She felt the ripples closing over her head. Was this how Irene was trapped?

Was it even her own home she stumbled into every night? Every house might have the same furniture, every door the same key.

No money. No money for a decent car, for friends and fun, for safety. Step off the tightrope, go ahead and try. Your worse enemies are in the same position, looking for weaker prey.

"The woman in that house was murdered!" That's what the man in the car at the bus stop had said. He was pointing at her door. He knew it was her door, they all knew she was the marked one. They only wondered if she knew it.

*   *   *   *

On the couch, in the afternoon, she dreamed again.

This apartment, explained the previous owner, comes with its own rabid dog. She kills off the tenants, but what the hell, they're always late with the rent. There's a man down the street who collects spare body parts, so it's really convenient.

Over here are the hidden passageways where he gains entrance. Barely big enough for a cockroach, but that's all he needs. He crawls across the food, leaving traces of drugs behind.

And he should be more careful with those unregulated street drugs. You never know what's in them.

*   *   *   *

There was no need for plans, for creeping through the dark holding a long sharp knife. He would come to her. On his own. Secretly, carefully concealing all he did. He would spring on her some dark empty night.

But she would be waiting.

A car went by. Silence.

She must have been drugged. She felt so very calm. Imagine calling the police when you were drugged. That wouldn't be intelligent, would it? Imagine trying to explain. Well first he stole the battery off my car and then he poisoned my dog and before that he killed his girl-friend Irene and that's what he was going to do with me.

You understand, don't you officer?

The neighborhood was quiet. As deserts are quiet. And graveyards.

If you look at it logically, she was trapped. She could not save her-self. No one would believe her. The bullies lived and the victims died and history was rewritten to suit the facts as they had turned out for the winners. They must be right. After all, they were alive, with the power of the living to create truth. The dead had no power.

And who did Irene leave her key with, when she went away on vaca-tion?

*   *   *   *

Rachel dug a grave for Merle in the backyard. It was a long job. Merle was a big dog. Her only protection, since she had no man.

"Help you bury your dog?"

She blinked at the man by the gate. He wouldn't quite come into focus. It was Joe, of course. Smug and confident, he came forward.

She felt very strange. Sunstroke, no doubt. Was this a good idea? said the voices, outraged.

The edge of the shovel caught Joe on the side of the head. He didn't fall down right away, so Rachel hit him a few more times, just to be sure.

*   *   *   *

There was a dead man right in the middle of her back yard. Next to him a big dead dog, decently covered with a sheet. The neighborhood was quiet around her, completely shocked by this turn of events.

She had stopped the voices cold.

No one could see over the fence. She continued to dig. Almost big enough now. Probably there was money in his wallet. Then she could take his key and go right in his house and help herself to anything. She would be his girlfriend. After all, she was the living one. She could make up any story she wanted to.

That was how it worked and she knew all about it now. To shut up the voices you had to have your own voice. You had to be the one to tell the story. You didn't let anybody else do that, or you would be part of their story and it wouldn't turn out right for you at all, in the end.

The Phantom of Kansas

Rachel passed the hitchhiker for the seventh time that night before she realized it was the same man.

It could be a coincidence, she told herself. She had only taken particular notice of him the last time she had passed him, noticed the beret and the backpack and the way his jeans were frayed. Hadn't she seen them all just an hour before? It was not so strange to pass a hitchhiker twice, even in the middle of the lonesome Kansas night. Someone might have picked him up, passed her, and set him down. After all her old Nova wasn't really up to highway speeds. But she had seen many hitchhikers that night, all thin young men.

Rachel had started six months ago by changing her name. She hadn't meant anything criminal by it, it was just that her luck had not been that good lately. Bill had decided it was all over, she had no job and no money, just the apartment, too expensive, and the phone bill and the electric bill and the car repair bill. She thought vaguely that changing her name might change her luck, fool the bad luck into leaving.

She had become Lisa Bell, a long-lost childhood friend, now safely married and living somewhere in the suburbs of Minneapolis. Ex-cheerleader, plump, blonde, mother, married to a pleasantly bland shoestore manager who came home every night to dinner on the table. Lisa was a comfortable person to be. She had stepped from point to point, home, school, marriage, without knowing how precarious it all was, how uncertain.

Besides, Lisa was a real person, with a real history the electric company could check on.

So far it wasn't working. It had been six months. Hard to believe it. Time had just slipped through Rachel's hands. At first she just thought she would meet a new man and things would come about the way they were supposed to. They would just fall into place. A cute guy with a good job and a nice car. But at the clubs they were so young, or so old, or so very married. Like Bill, they had that strange ability not to really see her at all.

Right now Lisa Bell was living in a trailer park on the edge of town. This was uncharacteristic of her, as Rachel recalled. She would have spent extra money for a small, comfortable apartment in some giant complex where there was a pool and a laundry room. There, in spite of her reduced circumstances, she would give little spaghetti dinner parties for her friends, one of whom would introduce her to the perfect man. But for now Lisa lived with cockroaches and greasy curtains and the miniature golf course across the highway.

In the shopping malls she saw the girls from high school with their short boyish hair and their slim boyish figures, wearing big shirts and witty shoes. Rachel used to be like them, back when Lisa was so plain and white-bread ridiculous. Slowly she had faded into a Walmart clerk, a bank teller, summer help in the library. With no effort at all she became a person who cut her own hair and whose shoes wore out before she got new ones. She ate hot dogs and peanut butter and watched soap operas on a small black and white TV. She worked nights.

Life was supposed to fall into place for her when she left Minnesota with Bill. Now she was trapped in Kansas, a state as flat as a graveyard, with the same shaved lawns.

The sirens went off at 1:30 PM. Tornado. They came regularly each spring, destroying small towns and trailer parks. Every schoolchild was taught proper procedure to cope with one. She had found a yellowing pamphlet in one of the kitchen drawers when she moved in.

There were Tornado Watches, when one was merely expected, and Tornado Alerts, when one had actually been spotted. Or maybe it was the other way around. There would be little moving bulletins on the TV and on-the-spot reports. "Yes Roger, you can see it in the sky just behind me." (Picture of a small, dark smudge in the sky.)

And every newscast showed trailers twisted like cheap tin sheeting.

Rachel had never actually seen a tornado, although every native claimed to have. She had been told that they were much rarer now. You still had to take them seriously. They could rip right through the heart of town and you'd never even hear them coming. Pay close attention to the storm warnings, do not scoff at empty skies.

People would race like jackrabbits to the basement, children curl up like hedgehogs in school hallways, stores empty out swiftly when the sirens started.

But still she had never seen one.

The sky was black and low, with a glow under it to the west. Spatters of rain fell. Rachel finished the dishes and left them to dry on the scarred linoleum. She never used to do the dishes right away, but finally the roaches got to be too much. She never looked at first, when she switched on the light in the kitchen at night.

It seemed too bright in the kitchen suddenly, like an auditorium. Rachel put on her sweater and went outside. The weather was waiting, not knowing what to do.

Her neighbor, Charlotte, was in the sand lot out front. She was thirty-five, a bleached blonde, and getting thinner every day. She looked like death already, grayish skin and sunken cheeks. Rachel didn't see how she could get any worse and still be alive. Char said the doctors didn't know what was wrong. Rachel thought she must have some fatal disease, like cancer or AIDS, but didn't want to frighten people off. Her husband, Bruce the Unemployed, generally sulked around the house mornings. He was scrawny with tattoos and a big mustache. Rachel thought he looked exactly like a rapist would, mean and unattractive. Almost every afternoon he would roar off in a pickup to play cards with his friends, spending Char's money. Char worked nights, like Rachel.

"Guess we're all going to die together, huh Lisa?"

Although she liked Char, Rachel had never told her her real name.

"Looks that way. Unless you want to dive into a ditch."

The ditch was the other place you were supposed to hide when the tornado went through, bouncing cars like tennis balls.

Char had lived in Kansas all her life and could remember three times a tornado had actually touched down in the city. Maybe four people had died altogether, but then the permanently maimed and paralyzed always got forgotten somehow.

"Don't see nothing, Looks spooky, but I don't see nothing."

Rachel looked too, but she wouldn't have recognized a funnel cloud if it were three feet away and roaring like a freight train. The wind kicked up and blew trash through the sandy lot. Bruce's dog started barking.

"Damn dog. I'm going to shoot it one day," said Char, eyeing it where it was tied to the back clothesline. "It's too damn mean. I let Bruce feed it. It'd like to take my hand off."

Bruce beat the dog regularly, but they didn't talk about that. Dogs are tougher than people, Rachel would tell herself, listening to Bruce yell and hit the dog with the belt. She despised herself for not doing anything about it. She didn't have a phone to call the ASPCA. Phones cost money. She could have gone across the street to the gas station, but he would have been done by the time anyone came. They would have to see it themselves, she didn't dare give her name.

Sometimes when Char was filling in days at the liquor store Bruce would loiter around out front and say hi. Once he had been walking by and glanced in her window while she was dressing. She was just pulling her hose on, luckily not showing anything. Their eyes had locked for a moment. After that she kept her curtains shut all the time.

"Want a beer?" Char pulled one out of her big fabric purse. She always carried a supply with her.

"Thanks. Where's Bruce?"

"Gone somewhere." She shrugged. "Can't say I care."

"Thought maybe he got a job."

"Him?" Char snorted. "He can't get a job. Won't even try anymore. That last job, they say he stole from the register. They spread that all over any time he tried to get another job."

"Could he sue or something?"

There were no tornado legends. They were just a fact of life.

She had no clear idea, that was the problem. The future had been vague, until finally life had become a matter of avoiding things. Avoiding Bruce, avoiding unemployment, avoiding bills. She needed a positive guiding principle. Like—Be Kind To Everyone. Take A Chance. Play The Percentages. One of those little sayings that help you pick your way through the minefield of life. So you could avoid the traps without even knowing what they were.

"No way, man. He did time. Nobody would take his word."

Did time? Did she mean like in jail? She tried turning the words around to see if Char could have meant something else. What had he been in jail for? Dare she ask?

Lisa certainly wouldn't have known anyone who had been in jail.

Char sighed. "It was supposed to be easier in town. That's why we moved back here. Maybe get on at an aircraft plant."

"Easier, yeah. I heard that." Rachel started to mention Bill, but remembered in time that Lisa had never lived with anyone. Rachel had come to Wichita with Bill, dropping out of college after two difficult and uninteresting semesters. It had been a great relief to quit, at first.

"Rents are a lot lower here," she said. "But so is my pay. It's a sink-hole. You can get in, but you never get out. I was on unemployment. People move out of town on unemployment. I never even had enough to pay my bills."

"That was your mistake," said Char. "Paying them."

"Yeah, I'm a fucking moron." Lisa would never have cussed like that. Maybe she was getting into character. It felt uncomfortable to act wrong. If she went on with it, moved into town like she had thought of doing, got the right boring friends, maybe then something would happen at last.

Rachel yawned. The beer was taking hold. "Let's go for a walk. The fields are nice. If I don't move around I'm going to pass out."

In the back of the lot was a little wooded area. A stream ran through a deep gully that filled right up to the top when it rained. There was a wide sewage pipe across it. Rachel took off her shoes, but Char ran right across.

"You're crazy, Char." They stepped onto the other bank. "You know, this would be the perfect spot to dump a body. They're always turning up on the edge of town. Derelicts, winos, senile old men who wander away from nursing homes to die of unknown causes."

"Girl, you are morbid."

"That's what working in a grocery store will do for you. Rickie actu-ally knew the family of that guy who was found out west. Wonder if they just took him for a walk when he got to be too much trouble."

Beyond the woods the fields were overgrown with tall grass.

"Is this wheat? It's kind of in rows."

"I wouldn't know wheat if it was growing in the front yard. Think we'll be hit by lightening, walking in the open like this?"

I've got rubber soles on my shoes."

"Shoot, girl. Lightning melt those right off your feet."

There was a scummy pond in the middle of the field. A dead rabbit was plopped on top of the mold a few feet from the edge. "Oh, gross. Want another beer?"

"Sure. What's that bunny doing out there? Didn't drown. Didn't get hit by a car. Didn't fly out there and die of starvation."

They stared in silence, trying to think of some logical explanation.

"Is it real spooky here all of a sudden?" whispered Char.

"The vengeful ghosts of murdered rabbits will rise again."

"Well, how did it get out there?"

"Maybe a dog killed it."

"A dog would eat it."

They stared for a few long moments.

"Let's get out of here."

They hurried back across the field.

"Look up there."

Something was swinging from a tree in the windbreak. It was too dark and high up to see clearly.

"Too small for a person."

"How about part of a person?" Rachel laughed doubtfully. "The rest could just have rotted off."

"Come on. You can't hang yourself on a branch that thin."

"Maybe a thin person could. He would have fallen off around here somewhere."

They poked around the tree, but found nothing.

"Might be an owl up there, I guess. I see feathers."

"What's it tied up there for?"

"Mad animal torturer on the loose."

"Sure climbs trees good."

"You know, a coyote could have carried off the rest."

"No coyotes around here, girl."

The tornado sirens chose that moment to go off again.

"Suuurrre there're coyotes. Hear them howl."

They laughed nervously and headed back home.

The drug addicts next to Charlotte's trailer had their stereo cranked up. There were two of them, a thin stringy one and a pale pudgy one. Rumor had it that they were gay. No woman had been seen to cross their threshold. They rarely went out and were said to live in filth and squalor.

Both of them were sitting on the front steps of their trailer when Char and Rachel came back.

"Howdy," said Rachel uncertainly. Lisa would never talk to such weirdos. She never asked for trouble like that. But then, she never had to live near them.

"You'all want a toke?"

Rachel blinked in surprise. They sure were easy, taking up with strangers like that.

"Sure," said Char. Why not? thought Rachel with annoyance. She was a dying woman anyway.

"Come on in."

Inside was every bit as bad as rumor had it. The curtains were drawn, pots were piled in the kitchen, old chairs with vinyl seats were in the living room, along with cartons of glasses and books. Dog chew toys were strewn all over the floor.

"Let me shut the door. Don't want the neighbors peeking in."

"We are the neighbors," said Rachel. Trapped with two drug addicts behind closed doors. It would end in tragedy. She should have known better, everyone would say. But it was hard to be rude at this point.

"Weird looking weather," said Sean, the thin one.

"Mass murder weather," said Rachel.

"She's so morbid," said Char.

The fat boy passed around a joint.

"What do you mean, morbid?" asked Rachel with feigned hurt. "There are all kinds of strange deaths out here. People just turning up dead. Unidentified people. People no one cares about. Usually a person gets killed by someone they know. This is just not normal."

"There were those two kids at Joyland," said Kurt. "That guy who jumped off the haunted house ride and slit their throats as they went through. They thought he was part of the exhibit."

"I heard that too," said Char. "A long time ago. I think it was just made up."

Rachel had heard about it. Their bodies had bobbed out the swinging wooden doors, creaking open to the light of day before horrified onlookers. The attendant panicked and shut down the ride, trapping six people inside with the maniac.

"They used to scare us in grade school with the Greenie Meanie. Some guy dressed all in green who used to hang around the playgrounds and tried to lure kids into his green car."

"Now that was probably true."

They sucked in the thick smoke, as the light grew brighter and brighter and the air grew more tangible. A ripped upholstered chair vibrated with menacing poverty.

"I gotta do the dishes…" said Char finally.

"Man, you sure do talk slow." They all laughed.

"It's the weed, man. It's treated."

"Come on, let's go."

"Stop by some time." Sean looked wistfully eager.

"Think they wanted a foursome?' asked Char outside.

"Which one would you do? Chubbo or Bones?"

They got more beer out of Char's fridge and used the bathroom. "Goddam, you got a case in here. Buy it by the truckload?"

"That's nothing. There's two more out back. Bruce drinks most of it, but I get my share."

"Hey, I got an idea. Let's play miniature golf."

Rain pattered lightly on the roof.

"You're crazy. It isn't even open."

"Sure it is. See the old guy watching the sky?"

"Hey. OK. What does it cost?"

"Three fifty. We have that?"

She had six quarters and Char produced two dollar bills. They staggered across the highway, talking loudly, four beers in Char's purse.

They spent over an hour knocking balls into puddles and through the arms of windmills. The old man who ran the place watched them nervously—he was drunk as a coot himself. No doubt afraid they would knock over a picket fence or a plastic flamingo right before his red inflamed eyes. There was a nervous smile on his face the entire time. But they were paying customers, after all.

At four they staggered back across the highway.

"Oh man, am I bombed. I hope I can make it to work."

"Call in sick."

"Can't. I need the money," said Rachel automatically. She couldn't bear to spend the evening in her trailer. Work wasn't better, but it was different.

"Oh shit, Bruce is back. I forgot about dinner. See you later."

Rachel heard him shouting as she got ready for work. "I don't ask much, just that my fucking dinner be ready—"

Rachel hurried out. She'd been late once already this week. It was never like this in the magazines—Mandy, a photographer's assistant, models our new spring line. Mandy weighs 102 pounds and her fiance is a successful playwright. They share a comfortable downtown loft and Mandy is studying theater—

Mandy is living in a trailer park.

Rain splattered across the windshield. The wipers weren't working right and smeared mud across the glass. The back window fogged up. She tried to drive carefully, unable to see a thing. At the grocery store she parked on the outskirts of the lot with the other employees and sprinted in.

Charlie, the manager, called her over when she clocked in. He was a short, balding man with a continually harassed expression. He was given to panic-stricken outbursts. The store wasn't showing much of a profit. Periodically he decided this was due to the dishonesty and inefficiency of the staff and fired half of them. Especially the black half. He felt this impressed those remaining with his stern authority.

It seemed to.

He sat back in his chair. "Jenny no longer works for this organization." Jenny was a cheerful black Mexican girl. Rachel had liked her. "There is no reason for her to be on the premises. If you see her notify the police or myself at once."

He looked at her significantly, but she did not ask the obvious questions. She was too used to it to be surprised. Satisfied that his announcement did not surprise her, Charlie sent her back to work.

She had survived two pogroms as Lisa Bell.

Two, so far.

"Quiet tonight," said Rickie, one of the sackers. He hoisted himself up on the counter with muscular arms. Rickie was fifteen if he was a day, black, and determinedly ignorant. "Did you hear about Jenny stealing?"

She snorted. "What makes you think she stole anything?"

"She's gone, ain't she? All that money in the drawer. Don't say you never thought about it."

"Wouldn't she be arrested if she did that?"

"She gave it back when she got caught."

"You sure know a lot about it. Were you there?"

"Nobody was there." He smiled winningly. "Hey, Princess, let's you and me go off in the back. Charlie's gone."

"Forget it, Rickie. I don't rob cradles."

"I ain't no baby. I'm a man. You a good-looking woman, Princess. You and me, we could go places."

"Like South Broadway?"

"No, man. I treat my ladies right."

She rolled her eyes and occupied herself with straightening out her station. She never knew whether to actually get mad at the guy or just laugh. Rickie actually looked disappointed, like he thought he had a chance. Prostitutes started out somewhere, she supposed. Why not in grocery stores? She could probably make Rickie a lot of money. What would seem like a lot of money to him. Enough to give him an edge.

It was right there in the cash drawer. Rickie's edge. Something to give him a start. But Rickie would never give him a shot at it. Charlie knew better. She was the one who double-checked the night's receipts and made out the bank deposit. And she knew what she had to lose.

Sure, she'd thought about it before, the way that you do. Not like it preyed on her mind though. What did it hurt? It was only idle speculation.

She wasn't a thief. The mere thought made her skin turn cold. Exposure. Prison. She wouldn't have the nerve. She couldn't do it.

But Lisa Bell could.

Lisa's life was running in adding machine columns in her head. Three-fifty rent, fifty utilities, two hundred food and gas. And repair bills. And things she wanted to buy. And one-eighty-nine fifty a week from Food-4-Less. And nothing better than Food-4-Less in this town. And without money, how would she ever get out?

She could put it off, think it over. But that was an excuse. She was scared to do it. She would just put it off until it was too late and then she would pretend she never had the chance.

A customer came by and so did Charlie, glaring at Rickie and smiling at the same time. Rickie jumped down hastily.

"Richard, could I see you in my office? When you have the time?"

Soon she would hear Rickie's high-pitched, protesting voice. But for now, everything had vanished with a high whine into the fluorescent lighting.

What was the big emergency? Why tonight? Why ever? A Jew in Germany, 1935. Things aren't so bad. It's home. Leaving is complex, expensive. But it was that magic stop moment when the restrictions were gone and the danger had not yet come.

The hours crept by. She bought herself a candy bar, paying for it at another station as per regulation. What was there to connect her to

Lisa? Over and over again she thought. But there was nothing. Lisa would vanish. Nasty little blonde bitch. Always knew it was just an act.

At 1:15 AM she gathered the cash drawers and receipts as usual and stayed behind, to balance them alone in the office. Theoretically Charlie was supposed to stay with her, but he never did.

She sat blankly in his confused, dreary, windowless office. She wasn't a thief. She didn't know what steps to take next. The door was propped open, hearing footsteps she realized she had to look normal to whoever walked by.

She began to balance the drawers. Lynn was a hundred dollars short. The very first one. She recounted the money in disbelief. Still short. Normally Charlie recounted the offages.

Lynn, this is your lucky day.

She proceeded as usual, strapping up the extra cash to be deposited, leaving some in the drawer. Then she realized that that was silly and took almost all of the large bills, strapping them haphazardly in bundles about the right size.

Charlie came in on the last box. Fighting for calm she counted and recounted the cash, waiting for him to leave. He pottered around.

"Any problems?"

"Almost done," she said, praying he wouldn't suddenly decide to check her work. Or notice how low the money was in the boxes. He nodded and wandered out the door.

Cosmic balance, Charlie. You said somebody stole and somebody did.

She should have six thousand in the bank deposit. She wavered before writing it down. If only she had paid more attention. Planned things out. She could have carried on for a week and gotten ten times as much.

The money was still on the table and she was fretting, she suddenly realized. She wrote down the correct amount and threw the slip in the bag with the fives and singles. Then she reached back in and pulled out a few small bills for change.

Time was running out. Her purse was in the car. She couldn't stuff it all in her pockets. How about the waistband of her pants? What if a bundle slipped out? What if it slipped out in front of Charlie? She saw the rubber bands then, and recalling some detective show, fastened them around her ankles. Several rubber bands for each bundle, in case one broke. Moving quickly, she threw the deposit bag in the safe and slammed the door. She left a copy of the deposit on the desk as usual.

Charlie was just coming in as she left.

"All done," she said. He grunted and ignored her.

Out the door and into the car. She dropped the keys three times, twice outside the car and once inside. She groped on the floor for them—of course the interior light was broken. Finally she got the car started. The money was hurting her ankles, so she pulled it off and tossed it on the floor, where it couldn't be seen by any passing trucks.

She turned and headed for the highway, away from the trailer park, the Food-4-Less, from the city. She knew better than to stop back home for anything.

She gassed up at an all-night station on the way out of town. Fifteen dollars. The little adding machine was going in her head again. Twenty a night for a tacky motel. Thirty more for food, gas, clothes. A hundred at least. How much did she have? She didn't dare stop and count.

Her mind was blank, her hands were shaking. She was heading west instinctively. Toward California, warmth and palm trees. Hollywood and serial murders.

Western towns, tiny and lonesome, slid by in the night. Big cities were expensive. San Diego, San Francisco, L.A. Don't stop. Don't think about it. She could figure out later how to get along there. People do it all the time.

She scrabbled the money off the floor as she was driving and pulled over on a deserted stretch of the road, under a streetlight. Keeping the motor running she sorted it, glancing in the mirror for headlights. She counted quickly and banded it in $500 bundles. $5348. She put $48 in her purse and started moving again. Where to put the rest? Hide it? Not in the car. She had to keep it with her. Not in her purse. Someone might snatch it. $500 under the floormat, just in case. The tens, they were bulky. The rest on her. In her underwear. Taped on her stomach. Masking tape, that was what she'd get. $1.48.

That was settled.

She'd use the $348 to get to California. She needed some other clothes. Food. She shouldn't eat in restaurants, they were expensive. Maybe stop in a grocery store along the way. Peanut butter and Pepsi. Five bucks worth would last her.

Funny, the worries of a criminal weren't as bad as her usual worries.

Western Kansas was as barren as a desert. The towns were maybe thirty miles apart, but that was just the turnoffs. Roads leading off to nowhere, as far as she could see. If she were more paranoid she might take them, roads with no Highway Patrol. But this was quicker. And they wouldn't know till Monday. No towns, just green and white signposts rising up and vanishing to her right. Overpasses ghostly bridges in the night. Temple pillars. Black land, the sky filled with stars.

Ghost stories, legends, came back to her. She and Bill and his friends used to drive down these roads, under the stars, smoking dope and telling scary stories.

Theorosa's Bridge, where Theorosa drowned her half-Indian children before throwing herself in. She missed one, and if you stood on the bridge and called "Theorosa! Theorosa! I'm your long lost child!" she would reach up from the depths and drag you in.

Strange, that story, but it almost sounded true. Especially about drowning the half-Indian children that no one would help her feed.

The gas was down to a quarter tank. She realized she hadn't seen a gas station in hours. Of course, there were all kinds of signs. Haviland—Gas, Food, Lodgings. Bucklin—Gas. But what would be open this time of night? She hardly dared stop until she was out of the state. Why hadn't she lied about the take? Bled off a little at a time until she had six thousand and could leave quietly? Charlie had never checked her figures. What if they had her license number? If they did, she was dead. They'd know who she was. They had handwriting samples. Fingerprints galore. But that only counted if they caught you. Why should they?

Of course, she could never now become a celebrity, out there in the golden sun of California. She'd be recognized and arrested.

She passed a man walking beside the road. A presentment came over her. Stop. Pick him up. Chances were being tossed her way by fate. He would be attractive, educated, escaping from his suffocating wealthy family who would eventually relent and reclaim him and his sweet new fiancee, Lisa.

She drove on. He could be a mad killer. She could be another nameless corpse, now that she was almost free.

She saw the blinding lights of the gas station-restaurant right off the highway. Might as well have a cup of coffee. She had never fallen asleep driving yet, but she had a long ways to go.

She patted at her little packets of money and transferred three hundred dollars to deep in her purse. No need to be an open invitation. She filled the tank and went into the restaurant. Ashamed to get just coffee, she ordered some eggs and toast. $6.75. I'll start worrying when the wallet is empty, she told herself. I'll still have money, there'll be time to plan. One thing at a time. Besides, I've been through a lot.

A few truckers in there eyed her and dismissed their hopes.

In the grungy bathroom she combed her hair and applied blusher. She still looked half dead. Maybe she'd stop on the other side of Denver. My brother is in the hospital in Utah, she told the mirror. I have to go see him. She'd have to start using her real name. Or a new one. Was there someone else she'd like to be?

Maybe if she slept during the day in one of those thirty dollar cheap motels they wouldn't be so frightening, with their shouting, drunken men.

She needed some fresh underwear. Already she felt grimy. She'd buy some before she stopped tomorrow morning. She wished she had a pencil and paper to figure out her expenses. Maybe she should buy a gun.

She went back and sat down at the counter. Two cups of coffee. She'd have to stop later. Oh well, it would break up the monotony.

A man sat next to her. A thin young man, balding prematurely, with the wire-rimmed glasses of a student. A lost student from 1974.

"Little cold out," he remarked.

"I guess," she replied. He looked harmless. He was tall, but she probably outweighed him.

"Lonely too. I've been walking since my ride turned off. I'm going to California to watch my brother's house while he's gone. He's got a great house. Real dark out there without the lights. Kind of scary."

"Oh?" She gave him the barest encouragement to continue. He could become annoying. She suddenly realized he was the man she'd seen walking beside the highway.

"There's a ghost out there, you know. Some woman found dead on a county road around here. Never found out who she really was. Fake ID. They say she drives up and down the highway, trying to get out of the county, but she never finds her way."

"Sounds like a real Midwest tragedy."

"Jesus is coming!" There was a ragged man in the doorway. He looked neither bathed or shaven. "He's coming for you!" He fixed them with crazed eyes. "Are you ready for him?"

The counter man stepped out and glared. "Get along, Joe, out you go."

The counter man came back in a minute. "They wander in every so often. Damned if I know where they come from. It's the highway, I guess. Not a town around for miles. There's Larned, where they keep the crazy people. But that's fifty miles away. I know the guy can't fly."

"We're at an outpost of reality," said the thin man. "The dark tides of night wash against the doors, but we keep it at bay. That is the function of these way stations, to keep out the forces of chaos. To keep the treadmill running smoothly. And you don't even know it."

"That's right, Bob," said the counterman. He seemed to make up names for people, as she had made up her own.

"Unknowing, dedicated servants, bred and trained from birth to detect the slightest sign of abnormality, here at the corner of the universe, where other realities might break in. When the door creaks open they are here to shove the dread creatures back into the outer chill."

"Maybe you would like to go back into the outer chill?"

The student shrugged, but shut up.

Here in the plains, where time runs slower, where there are areas a human being might not visit for a hundred years, it's easy to cross over. Out that door you might find nuclear devastation, a primal swamp. The restaurant had always been here and always would be. The Indians themselves have forgotten what was here before it.

Rituals abound. Churches and gas stations and bingo parlors. Laundromats. None of it with any meaning, except to keep out the strange and the stranger.

Back in Wichita the trailer was dark. A dog howled.

And Rachel awoke and it was all a dream.

No, even then she would do the same. She would take the money. Even if it was a relief to wake up and know she had done nothing wrong.

The night was silent, waiting for the things you see, but never hear about, the things you hear about, but never see.

Seven times she had passed him on the road that night. Appointment in Samarra. You can't outrun your fate, they say.

But you don't have to stop for it either.

0-595-25374-1